MASSACRE IN MOOSE CITY

ACRE IN MOOSE CITY

x and his war party stage a
s attack on the Oregon township
se City and abduct Rebecca,
r of Mayor Andrew Lucas. Accom-
by the Kentuckian gunfighter Jack
Lucas and the deputy marshal set off
suit of the kidnappers.

ree men are tested to the limit for
ve to face not only Crazy Fox and his
but also a couple of unscrupulous
ters.

MASSACRE IN MOOSE CITY

by

J. D. Kincaid

Dales Large Print Books
Long Preston, North Yorkshire,
BD23 4ND, England.

British Library Cataloguing in Publication Data.

Kincaid, J. D.
　　Massacre in Moose City.

　　A catalogue record of this book is
　　available from the British Library

　　ISBN　1-84262-019-3 pbk

First published in Great Britain by Robert Hale Limited, 1999

Copyright © J. D. Kincaid, 1999

Cover illustration © FABA by arrangement with
Norma Editorial S. A.

The right of J. D. Kincaid to be identified as the author of this
work has been asserted by him in accordance with the
Copyright, Designs and Patents Act, 1988

Published in Large Print 2000 by arrangement with
Robert Hale Ltd.

Dales Large Print is an imprint of Library Magna Books Ltd.

Printed and bound in Great Britain by
T.J. (International) Ltd., Cornwall, PL28 8RW

ONE

It was April in the year of Our Lord 1878, and the snows still blocked the high passes through the Blue Mountains. On the second Sunday of the month, a chill wind whistled down Main Street, Moose City, a small prairie township in Fairfield County, in the State of Oregon. Winter had not yet admitted defeat and given way to Spring.

The clock struck twelve and the congregation began to emerge from Moose City's recently constructed, wooden-framed church.

The first person to appear was the Reverend Martin Ross, for it was his duty to shake hands with each and every member of his flock as he or she left the building.

A tall, broad-shouldered man in his late thirties, with strong, resolute features and wise, kindly brown eyes, the minister was hatless and dressed in clerical attire. His thick brown hair was ruffled by the northerly wind and he shivered slightly. Although Moose City itself was clear of snow, there remained patches scattered here and there across the plain that lay to the west of the township, and also amongst the foothills and ravines situated to the east, between it and the mountain range. The reverend gentleman prayed for a change of wind, as he turned to speak to the first of the congregation to leave the church.

''Mornin', Andrew. Nice to see you an' Naomi both, an' Rebecca.'

'Yes. Wa'al, don't forgit, Reverend, you're invited to lunch,' replied Andrew Lucas.

'I surely won't. Lookin' forward to it,' replied Ross, with a smile.

Andrew Lucas nodded and passed on, followed by his wife and daughter. He was Moose City's present mayor and the grandson of its founder, Abraham Lucas.

Forty years old, Lucas had a thin,

patrician face and piercing blue eyes, with grey-flecked black hair and a grey moustache and goatee. In his expensive, black, three-piece, city-style suit, he cut a dapper figure, for he was of no more than medium height and of slender build.

Naomi Lucas was of a similar age and had worn her years well. A pretty, blonde-haired woman, in a smart dark green velvet gown and bonnet, she was no less elegant than her husband.

The third person to shake the minister's hand was their 17-year-old daughter, Rebecca. She had inherited her mother's blonde hair and her father's blue eyes. Slim and petite, Rebecca had a lovely oval face and a sunny smile. Her fine young figure, with its tiny waist and small, firm breasts, was encased in a blue-and-white check cotton dress, and she wore a wide-brimmed straw-hat. All in all, she presented a picture of exceptional beauty.

The next to emerge from the church were Lawrence Baird and his family. Baird was a lawyer and Moose City's second citizen. A tall, lean, elegant man, he had a handsome yet rather sombre face. He was Lucas's contemporary and, like him, sported a splendid three-piece city-style suit, though in a light grey. His wife, Margaret, was a pretty, plump woman in blue velvet, and they had two pretty young daughters, and a good-looking 18-year-old son, Luke.

Following this family was Doc Barton, a small, elderly, balding, bespectacled bachelor, scruffily attired in a well-worn beige jacket and rumpled grey trousers. After taking his leave of the Reverend Martin Ross, he turned and began a conversation with Nathaniel Peabody, the town mortician, tall and lugubrious in stovepipe hat and long black coat.

The mortician's wife and three daughters succeeded Peabody on the church porch. Then came Henry Rolls, the white-haired, 50-year-old owner of the general store, with his wife and family, and, after him, the proprietor of the town's only hotel and also the livery-stables, big, pot-bellied, red-faced Frank Bingham.

Other families followed, and it was some time before the church eventually emptied, for, apart from Sam Brand and his girls at the Lucky Strike Saloon, and a few ne'er-do-wells, almost the entire population of Moose City, together the vast majority of the homesteaders in that part of Fairfield County, invariably attended church on a Sunday morning.

Indeed, there were even some cowboys in attendance, for half-a-dozen of the Lazy S's hands had accompanied their boss, Dale Stewart, his wife and four children to church that morning. They were next-to-last to leave, for Stewart habitually occupied the foremost pew, which precluded an early departure.

'Fine sermon, Reverend,' declared the rancher genially, as he shook Ross's hand. 'Jest hope them boys o' mine was payin' attention.'

This remark referred not to Stewart's two

sons, but to his hands, for the minister had been preaching in no uncertain terms about the sins of the flesh, and, in common with most cowboys, the Lazy S's hands were not averse to a little drinking, gambling and whoring.

Dale Stewart, a tall and broad-shouldered, rawboned man in his late thirties, was one of the few in church that morning to be carrying a gun. Although dressed in his Sunday best – low-crowned black Stetson, cambric shirt with ruffed collar, black Prince Albert coat, dark grey trousers and gleaming black leather boots – he still packed a Colt Peacemaker. So did his six hands, for there had been rumours that a band of renegade Snake Indians was on the warpath and had been spotted heading in the direction of Fairfield County.

The last to leave the church was also carrying a Colt Peacemaker. He was Lew Jackson, Moose City's 19-year-old deputy marshal, a tall, gangling youth, with a frank, good-natured face and a quiet resolve to do his best to maintain law and order in the township. He had no Sunday best and, consequently, wore his everyday clothes: an ill-fitting brown jacket, threadbare white cotton shirt, brown bootlace tie, grey trousers and highly polished but well-worn boots. He plonked a battered grey Stetson on his head, as he bade the minister good morning and stepped off the church porch and into Main Street.

A few minutes earlier, the town had been practically deserted, but now Main Street was crowded, with various families heading from the church to home and lunch. The homesteaders were either on horseback or in gigs or buckboards, trotting down Main Street towards the plain. Dale Stewart drove a four-wheeled carriage, flanked by two of his hands, foreman Jim Beaton and wrangler Pete Gordon. The other four were on their way to the Lucky Strike Saloon, as were Doc Barton, Nathaniel Peabody and a few other of Moose City's menfolk.

Doc Barton liked to remark that he was

'thirstin' after righteousness', a joke, which, since he insisted upon making it every Sunday, had grown somewhat thin.

Lew Jackson, for his part, was neither heading towards the saloon nor home for lunch. He was about to commence duty, taking over from Marshal Ben Langley, who was awaiting his arrival at the law office.

Langley stood on the sidewalk outside the office, smoking a large, fat cigar. He was a stout, heavy-jowled man in his mid-forties, who had served the town well over the years, but was a deal less active these days. He waddled rather than walked, and the buttons on his check shirt threatened to pop at any moment. As for his brown leather vest, to which was pinned his marshal's badge, that had remained unbuttoned for some months past. A brown Stetson, faded blue denim pants and brown leather boots completed his attire, and he, too, carried a Colt Peacemaker.

'Hi, Lew,' he growled. 'Was the Reverend on good form this mornin'?'

'Sure was. Sermon was full of hell-fire an' damnation,' said Lew Jackson cheerfully.

'That's the kinda sermon I 'preciate,' stated Langley.

'Then you oughta go to church some Sunday,' said Lew Jackson.

'Cain't. My duty keeps me here,' replied the marshal.

'We could swop duties. You could go to church an' I–'

'No! No!' declared Langley. 'Cain't have you missin' church, Lew. That wouldn't do at all.'

'But–'

'You're young an' impressionable. You need churchin', whereas I...'

But Marshal Ben Langley got no further, for he was interrupted by a bloodcurdling screech and, moments later, a band of Snake Indians galloped into the town from the east. They had swooped down through Powder Pass, half a mile away, ridden hell-for-leather across the intervening scrubland and hit Moose City before anyone had an inkling that they were even in the neigh-bourhood.

There were a score or more, led by Crazy Fox, a stocky, powerfully built brave riding a coal-black racing-pony. His black eyes glinted fiercely and his face, with its large hooked nose, high cheekbones and wide, cruel mouth, looked decidedly satanic, smeared, as it was, in black war paint. He wore half-a-dozen eagle feathers in his head-dress and the bells sewn into his buckskins were all a-jangling. His long black hair streamed out behind him, as he galloped along Main Street, screeching maniacally and shooting down the citizenry. He blazed away with his Colt Peacemaker and then, when he had emptied the revolver, he pulled a Winchester from his saddle-boot and began firing the rifle into the populace, who, panic-stricken were running for cover.

The renegade Snake Indians could not have struck at a worse time, for Moose City's townsfolk were, for the most part, unarmed and, in the immediate aftermath of the church service, thronging Main Street. Only Dale Stewart and his hands, and the two lawmen, were in a position to respond. They fired back at the Indians, but hastily and inaccurately as they, like the others, desperately sought shelter.

Dale Stewart drove the buckboard down the alleyway between the livery-stables and Henry Rolls' general store, while Jim Beaton and Pete Gordon leapt from their horses and threw themselves behind a couple of large barrels which stood on the sidewalk in front of the store. Their fellow hands were less fortunate. All four were cut down before they could reach the safety of the Lucky Strike Saloon. Doc Barton, Nathaniel Peabody and a couple of other townsmen did, however, succeed in diving in through its bat-wing doors.

Henry Rolls was shot dead on the threshold of his store, though his wife managed to push the children inside. Frank Bingham, for his part, had his skull split open by a tomahawk, as did several others, as some of the Indians, upon emptying their revolvers or rifles, resorted to either tomahawk, lance or knife.

Shooting, stabbing and hacking indiscriminately and, all the while, screeching their savage war cries, the renegade Snakes continued to terrorize and massacre the townsfolk; men, women and children.

The saloon-keeper, Sam Brand, made the mistake of peering out through one of the saloon windows. A chance shot shattered the pane and buried itself in his chest. Coughing up blood, he collapsed in a heap, where he was attended by Doc Barton. But there was nothing the physician could do, for the wound was mortal.

Upstairs, another denizen of the saloon made a similar fatal error. Sadie Juniper, a voluptuous, green-eyed red-head, who, at twenty years old, was the youngest of Sam Brand's sporting women, rose from her bed upon hearing the cacophony of screeches, screams and shots outside. Curiosity impelled her towards the window. She peered out and, as she did so, Crazy Fox looked up, took swift aim and fired his Winchester. The bullet pierced the girl's forehead and, with a sharp cry, she fell backwards, knocking over a chair as she crashed to the floor.

Her male companion leapt from the bed with an angry curse. He dropped down beside the girl, but realized at once that she was beyond help. The bullet had lodged in Sadie Juniper's brain and killed her instantly.

Jack Stone continued to curse. He had ridden into town the previous night, looking for food, drink and a bed for the night. Sharing that bed with the voluptuous redhead had been a bonus. And now she was dead. He swore loud and long, then crept across to the window and peered cautiously above the sill. What he saw sickened him. The street was littered with the bodies of dead and wounded men, women and children, and still the carnage went on. While he watched, Marshal Ben Langley was hit as he attempted to go to the aid of a couple of badly wounded children. Three slugs slammed into the lawman's stout frame, lifting him off his feet and depositing him on his back in the middle of the street.

Stone waited to see no more. He retraced his steps and hurriedly began to dress. Six foot two inches in his stocking-feet and comprising two hundred pounds of muscle and bone, the Kentuckian presented a formidable figure. His craggy, square-cut face, with its deep-set, pale blue eyes and broken nose, had been handsome once and, when he smiled, regained something of its former good looks. But he was not smiling now.

He pulled on his grey shirt, faded blue denim pants and well-worn, unspurred boots. Then he tied a red kerchief round his thick, strong neck, fastened on the gunbelt and holster carrying his Frontier Model Colt and shrugged on his knee-length buckskin jacket. Next, he roughly brushed his grey-flecked brown hair before donning a grey Stetson. And, finally, he grabbed the Winchester from where it stood, propped against a bedside cabinet, and quickly left the room.

While Stone was still on his way downstairs, the massacre continued unabated outside in Main Street, the Snake Indians by now in a frenzy of bloodlust.

Amongst those still alive and unhurt, Rebecca Lucas found herself separated from her mother and father. She had been about fifty yards behind her parents when the attack commenced. They had been talking with Lawrence and Margaret Baird, while she had fallen back to chat to the two Baird girls and their brother, Luke. In their panic, the four youngsters all promptly set off in different directions.

Rebecca, spying four young children ahead of her, hustled them down an alleyway between the barbering parlour and the mortician's premises, almost exactly opposite the alleyway down which Dale Stewart and his family had escaped a few minutes earlier. But she was not so lucky, for one of the Snake braves spotted her disappearing down the alley.

Dancing Fox, at twenty-one Crazy Fox's younger brother by three years, wheeled his pony round and set off in pursuit. Slightly taller and slimmer than the renegade leader, he was similarly attired and armed, and his lean, cruel features were also smeared with black war paint. Indeed, he presented no less frightening a figure than did Crazy Fox himself

The children screamed as the Indian bore down on them. With eyes wide with terror and their faces blanched of all colour, they huddled round Rebecca for protection. The girl did her best to calm her own fears and courageously stepped between the children and the fast-approaching brave.

He let loose a bloodcurdling screech and, bending low over the pony's neck, grasped hold of the girl, lifted her off her feet and threw her across its back in front of him. And there he held her in a grip of iron.

22

Rebecca struggled and screamed, but to no avail. Dancing Fox pulled the tomahawk from his belt and struck her a sharp blow behind the left ear, rendering her senseless. Then, ignoring the cowering, sobbing children, he again wheeled the pony round and galloped back down the alley, and out once more into Main Street.

As Dancing Fox rejoined his fellow renegades, a bugle sounded and a troop of US Cavalry suddenly appeared at the western end of the town. They were from nearby Fort Franklin and were led by Lieutenant Hugh Freeman, a young officer whose zeal unquestionably outweighed his experience. He drew his sword and led the charge down Main Street. But the sounding of the bugle had been a mistake, for it had alerted the Snake Indians. Consequently, before Freeman and his troopers could reach and engage them, they fled as swiftly as they had come. And, since the street was littered with the dead, the dying and the wounded, the troopers were forced to rein in their horses and come to a halt. As a result, Crazy Fox and his band made their escape with ease. They left the town in a cloud of dust, sped across the half-mile of scrubland and then vanished up Powder Pass.

The last to disappear up the pass was Dancing Fox, for he was slowed down by having the unconscious form of Rebecca Lucas draped across the pony's back. Nevertheless, he, too, escaped without any trouble, although some fifty or so yards behind the rest of the renegade band.

Lieutenant Hugh Freeman surveyed the dreadful scene. A tall, dark-haired subaltern in his early twenties, Freeman had seen little or no action before arriving at Fort Franklin. His handsome features were etched with horror at the sight of the carnage. He turned to his sergeant, Joe McGill, a stocky, square-jawed veteran of some forty summers. McGill had short-cut, iron-grey hair beneath his army cap and his tough, well-weathered features were completely impassive. He had seen such scenes before, and he recalled it had not always been the white folk who had been the ones to be slaughtered.

'See to it, Sergeant, that the men do what they can to help the wounded,' barked Freeman.

'Very good, sir,' replied the sergeant.

Then began, under McGill's instructions, an evacuation of the wounded from the street to the bar-room of the Lucky Strike Saloon. There they were laid out and tended to by Doc Barton, aided by several ladies of the town.

While this was going on, Andrew Lucas, Lawrence Baird and the Reverend Martin Ross organized the transportation of the dead to Nathaniel Peabody's funeral parlour. Amongst those who helped in this unhappy task was Jack Stone. And the first corpse the Kentuckian conveyed to the funeral parlour was that of the saloon girl, Sadie Juniper.

A tally was quickly made, and it was

ascertained that no fewer than fifty of Moose City's townsfolk were dead and thirteen wounded. Only two Indians had perished during the attack, one shot by Deputy Marshal Lew Jackson and one by the rancher Dale Stewart. The attack had lasted only a few minutes, yet the result was nothing short of a massacre.

Once the last of the wounded had been given into Doc Barton's care, the troopers immediately re-grouped and re-mounted. Before Lieutenant Hugh Freeman could give the order to ride out, however, he found himself confronted by Andrew Lucas, Lawrence Baird and the clergyman.

'Who in tarnation were those goddam savages?' demanded Lucas angrily.

'Yes, who were they? I thought all the Injuns hereabouts were confined to their reservation, a coupla miles south of Fort Franklin,' added Baird.

'That's right,' replied the subaltern.

'Then who–?' began Lucas.

'A bunch of young bucks, led by a mad,

murderin' sonofabitch named Crazy Fox, have broken loose and are on the warpath across this and neighbouring counties,' explained Freeman. 'Ain't that right, Sergeant?'

'Yessir,' affirmed McGill 'They've hit ranches, farms an' homesteads from Pendleton right down to the Harney Basin. But this is the first township they've attacked. If only we'd got here sooner!'

'Yes, indeed!' said Freeman. 'For we've been on their trail for some days now.'

'Have all the attacks been so – so bloodthirsty, so barbarous?' enquired the Reverend Ross.

'They certainly have,' said Freeman.

'I wonder why,' murmured Ross.

''Cause they're savages, that's why,' snarled Baird.

'I s'pose,' said the clergyman, 'though it's hard to comprehend. I mean, I can under-stand a bunch of young bucks findin' the confines of the reservation too restrictin', an' breakin' free, yet this...'

Amongst the crowd that had gathered was the Kentuckian, Jack Stone. He now spoke.

'A coupla years back, jest before the Snakes signed the peace treaty that restricted them forever to livin' on a reservation, a troop of drunken bluecoats raided Crazy Fox's village an' raped an' murdered several young squaws, Crazy Fox's wife amongst 'em.'

Hugh Freeman eyed Stone with ill-disguised fury

'That's a goddam lie!' he cried angrily.

'It's what I've heard more 'n once,' replied Stone quietly.

'Still, two wrongs don't make a right,' said Ross.

'Didn't say they did,' drawled Stone. 'But this would sure explain the savagery of the Injuns' attack.'

'It's a goddam lie, I tell you!' reiterated Freeman.

'So yuh keep sayin'. But, anyways, whatever the rights an' wrongs of the matter, I figure Crazy Fox an' his band gotta be stopped. They have got theirselves a taste for blood an' ain't likely to cry halt of their own accord. So,' said Stone, 'what's detainin' you, Lieutenant?'

'Nothing!' rasped Freeman and, with a wave of his gloved hand, he cried, 'Let's ride, men! Let's go git those murdering red bastards!'

Thereupon, as the crowd quickly parted, Freeman, his sergeant and the rest of the troop set off at a gallop. They soon cleared the town limits, then headed across the intervening scrubland, before finally disappearing into the deep ravine known as Powder Pass.

Once the soldiers had gone from view, Andrew Lucas turned to confront the Kentuckian.

'You seem to know a lot 'bout them goddam Snake Injuns,' he remarked.

'It's only what I've heard durin' my travels,' replied Stone. 'I've been doin' a li'l huntin' up in the Blue Mountains, y'see.'

'You don't come from these parts, though,

29

do yuh?' enquired Lawrence Baird perceptively.

'Nope. I hail from Kentucky. But I've been a rover most of my life.'

'Is that a fact, Mister ... er...?'

'Stone. Jack Stone.'

'Jack Stone!' Lew Jackson exclaimed and his eyes lit up. 'You – you ain't the same Jack Stone who stood side by side with Bat Masterson in Dodge City, an' – an' the man who tamed Mallory?' he asked excitedly.

Stone's exploits as a law officer were legion, but these days he was looking for a quiet life. He preferred to remain anonymous. He had hoped that his name would have remained unrecognized in this remote Oregon township.

'Marshal Langley told me 'bout you,' explained the young deputy.

'Yeah, I knew Ben in the old days,' said Stone. 'I saw him git hisself shot, so I guess you're marshal now,' he commented, glancing at the badge pinned to the pocket of the youth's ill-fitting brown jacket.

'Yeah. Guess so,' said the youngster rather sheepishly.

'Wa'al, Mr Stone, I'd best introduce myself,' said Lucas. 'I'm the mayor of this here town. Andrew Lucas.'

So began a round of introductions, at the end of which Stone knew by name the mayor, the lawyer, the minister and the town's new 19-year-old marshal. Before any further discussion could begin, however, Naomi Lucas and Margaret Ross came bustling up, dragging with them a tearful 9-year-old girl.

'Andrew! Andrew!' cried Naomi. 'I've been lookin' jest everywhere for Rebecca!'

'Wa'al, she's gotta be around someplace.'

'No, Andrew.'

'Yuh – yuh don't mean she's dead?'

'No. She's been taken.'

'Taken, Naomi?'

'By one of them Injuns. You tell him, Nancy.'

The little 9-year-old gazed up at the mayor through tear-filled eyes. 'I'm sorry,

Mr Lucas,' she wailed, 'but Rebecca, she tried to save me an' my friends from this awful redskin. He bore down on us, an' he grabbed Rebecca an' rode off with her.'

'Oh, no!'

'Yes, Mr Lucas. It's the truth.'

'Oh, sweet Jesus!' Lucas made no attempt to apologize for his words to the minister, but merely said, 'I – I must go after her.'

'The soldiers will surely save her, Andrew,' said the Reverend Ross, for his part discreetly ignoring the other's profanity.

'Mebbe, Mebbe not. Their main aim is to hunt down an' kill the Injuns, not to rescue Rebecca. 'Deed they don't even know she's been taken.'

'You're right, Andrew. I'll ride with you,' said Lawrence Baird.

'No,' said Lucas. 'You're needed here. To organize things in my absence.'

'But...'

'Doc Barton will probably need further medical supplies, an' some of the wounded may need transportin' to the hospital over in

Mitchell. Someone's gotta take charge of these matters.'

'Wa'al...'

'Mr Lucas is right. I'll ride with him,' volunteered Lew Jackson.

'But, as Mr Stone jest remarked, you're now town marshal. Your responsibilities are here in Moose City,' stated Lucas.

'I've also got a responsibility to bring those murderin' savages to justice,' rasped Lew Jackson, adding firmly, 'So, I'm comin'. Jest try an' stop me!'

'Wa'al, if'n you're determined?'

'I am.'

'Then let's go git saddled up,' said Lucas.

As the two men turned to head towards the livery-stables, the Kentuckian remarked quietly, 'I'll join you. Reckon yuh might need an experienced tracker, an' I was once an Army scout.'

'But this ain't your affair, Mr Stone!' protested Lucas.

'I'm makin' it my affair,' said the Kentuckian.

'Wa'al, we certainly would welcome you ridin' along with us,' declared the mayor.

'Then that's settled.'

Jack Stone smiled grimly. These days, he avoided trouble wherever possible, and he had no real inclination to become embroiled in the pursuit of Crazy Fox and his band of renegade Snakes. Yet, having witnessed the terrible slaughter on Moose City's Main Street, he felt he could not do otherwise than offer his services. Crazy Fox had to be tracked down and killed before he perpetrated any further massacres.

The three men hurried away and, within a matter of a few minutes, were saddled up and ready to ride. Thereupon, Andrew Lucas bade his wife a fond farewell and they galloped off in the wake of Lieutenant Hugh Freeman and his troop of US Cavalry. The chase was on.

TWO

Dancing Fox fell further and further behind the others as Crazy Fox and his band proceeded ever deeper into the Blue Mountains. Although Rebecca was only a little over eight stone, this additional weight had told on Dancing Fox's pony, and the animal had been unable to keep pace with the other braves' steeds. This did not trouble Dancing Fox, however, since there was, so far at least, no sign of the pursuing troop of US Cavalry. That they were on the Indians' trail he did not doubt, but the territory leading up into the mountains was wild and untamed, shrouded in forest and dissected by numerous deep gorges and ravines. To lose their pursuers would be an easy task. The band of Snake Indians need only split up and make for their camp high in the mountains by a variety of diverse routes.

As these thoughts were flitting through the Indian's brain, his captive suddenly began to stir.

Dancing Fox smiled. He would let his brother and the others pursue the course they were taking. He, in the meantime, meant to take a separate route, for he had something in mind to do, and had no wish to be interrupted by the arrival of the bluecoats. Consequently, he turned off the main trail and headed up into a narrow gorge to his left.

Once he had vanished from the view of anyone following his original trail, Dancing Fox reined in the pony. The girl had by now regained consciousness. She turned her head and, gazing up at her captor, let out a scream of terror. Dancing Fox laughed harshly, leapt from the saddle and threw Rebecca onto the dusty, sparsely grassed floor of the gorge. His wild black eyes devoured her lovely young body. Dancing Fox's bloodlust had been replaced by a lust of quite another kind.

He pinned the girl to the ground and thrust one hand up inside her skirt, while the other fondled her firm young breasts. Rebecca cried out and struggled desperately to free herself. To no avail. She could not match the Indian's brute strength. She was still screaming when the first of the two shots rang out. She had barely ceased when the second struck Dancing Fox and he pitched forward on top of her.

Rebecca lay shocked and stunned beneath the Indian. Then, all at once, he was rolled to one side and she found herself gazing up into the innocent blue eyes and fresh face of a 20-year-old youngster. Behind him, and still mounted, were two other males.

Rebecca studied the three men as she clambered to her feet. The youngster wore a lowcrowned grey Stetson, grey shirt, brown leather vest and levis, and he carried a Colt Peacemaker in a holster tied down on his right thigh. His two companions were some years older.

The taller of the pair was a rake-thin man with lank black hair hanging almost to his shoulders. His features were distinctly unprepossessing. He had a thin face with a long nose and narrow jaw. His eyes were close-set and as cold and hard as black pebbles, and he sported a black, pencil-thin moustache above his cruel rat-trap of a mouth. He was expensively attired in a knee-length black coat and black trousers, white cambric shirt and grey silk cravat and doeskin boots. A black stovepipe hat was clamped at a jaunty angle on his head and, as the girl watched him, he returned a pair of pearl-handled British Tranters to their respective holsters. It was he who had despatched Dancing Fox, with one shot slamming into the small of the Indian's back and the other blasting a hole in the back of his skull.

The second rider was a big, rawboned ruffian with brooding blue eyes. A bushy brown beard and whiskers pretty well disguised the pockmarks that dotted his face, but could not hide the livid white scar running diagonally across his forehead. He was similarly attired to the youngster, except that his leather vest was black and he carried a Remington in place of the other's Colt.

The youngster smiled gently at Rebecca.

'Guess we arrived in the nick of time, Miss,' he said.

'Yes. Yes, thank you,' gasped the girl. 'I – I am eternally in your debt.'

'It weren't nuthin'. We could scarcely have jest ridden on by, now could we?'

'You saved me from – from' Rebecca stuttered and stumbled to a halt, too flustered to continue.

'Yes, wa'al, let me introduce myself an' my friends,' interposed the youngster, sensing the girl's embarrassment. 'I'm Billy Malone and these here are Mr Danny O'Hare an' Mr Jake Rough.'

'P-pleased to meet you, Mr Malone; an' you, too, Mr O'Hare an' Mr Rough,' said Rebecca.

'You don't have to call me "mister". Billy'll do fine,' replied the youth amiably.

'Likewise, you jest call me Jake,' growled the bearded ruffian.

'Me, you'd best call Two-gun,' rasped the rake-thin gunman, Danny O'Hare. 'Most folks do,' he added with a grin.

'How – how do you do? I – I am Rebecca Lucas,' said the girl.

'Wa'al, Miss Lucas, would yuh care to tell us how you happened to be here in this godforsaken spot with that thar' Snake Injun?' enquired Billy Malone.

'Certainly,' said Rebecca and she went on to recount the terrible events of that Sabbath day. Tears flowed unashamedly down her cheeks as she described the massacre in Moose City, and she concluded her narrative with an account of how Dancing Fox had pursued her down an alley, knocked her unconscious and carried her off. 'My ma an' my pa will be jest frantic with worry!' she exclaimed.

'An' who might they be?' asked Two-gun

O'Hare, eyeing the girl with interest.

'My pa, he's the mayor of Moose City,' said Rebecca proudly.

'Is that so?' The gunman whistled, and an evil leer split his ugly features. 'Now ain't that somethin'?' he remarked.

'Sure is,' grinned Jake Rough.

'Pa will be sure to reward you for bringin' me safely home,' cried Rebecca eagerly.

'I s'pose he will,' said O'Hare. 'Whaddya say, fellers? Do we deliver Miss Lucas safely back to Moose City an' the bosom of her family?'

'Sure thing,' stated Billy Malone.

'Wa'al, I dunno,' said Rough, his face fixed on Rebecca's firm young breasts, as they rose and fell beneath the blue-and-white cotton dress. 'Mebbe there ain't no real hurry.'

'What have yuh in mind, Jake?' asked O'Hare with another grin.

'I was thinkin' that mebbe that Injun had the right idea.'

'What?' gasped Rebecca and then, as the

full meaning of Jake Rough's words dawned upon her, she cried, 'No! You cain't mean...'

'You – you ain't proposin' to – to—?' Billy Malone paused. He found that, like the girl, he couldn't bring himself to utter the words.

'Reckon we can have ourselves a li'l fun with Miss Lucas *and* claim our reward off her pa,' said Rough.

'Yeah. Why not?' smiled O'Hare.

'But, fellers...' began Billy Malone.

'But nuthin', Billy,' snapped O'Hare. 'Are you with us on this, or not?'

The youngster was nobody's fool, and he had no intention of setting himself at odds with his two companions.

'I – I'm with you, Two-gun. 'Course I am. I'm jest worried Mr Lucas won't part with no reward if'n we do this to his daughter. On the other hand, should we deliver her safe an' sound...'

'We don't hand her over till after Lucas has paid up,' said Rough.

'But, even so...'

'I told yuh, there ain't no buts, Billy. Jake's

right. Lucas will pay for his daughter, damaged goods or no. Hell, he might even be persuaded to pay a li'l extra when he realizes the kinda fellers he's dealin' with!' said O'Hare.

'That's right!' laughed Rough.

'Wa'al,' cried O'Hare, 'who's gonna have her first?'

'No! No, please! You – you cain't! You – you wouldn't!'

As the frightened girl backed away, her face the colour of chalk and her eyes filled with terror and revulsion, Billy Malone stepped between her and the two riders, who, at that moment, were about to dismount. He turned and faced them.

'Two-gun! Jake!' he cried. 'Let's not rush things. Yo're right. We can have our fun with Miss Lucas an' collect a nice, fat reward. But why not wait awhile? We could ride over to Trader Tait's place an' rent a room with a nice, comfortable bed. There it'd be–'

'Here's fine with me,' growled Jake Rough.

'There's every chance we could be interrupted,' declared the youngster.

'In this outa-the-way spot?' sneered Rough.

'Supposin' the Injuns have been pursued.'

'By who, for Pete's sake? Accordin' to Miss Lucas, a whole heap of folks was massacred. The survivors sure ain't likely to venture after 'em,' opined Two-gun O'Hare.

'No. But we don't know the circumstances of the Snake Injuns leavin' Moose City.'

'Wa'al, so whaddya say to that?' demanded O'Hare, glowering at Rebecca.

'I – I dunno. I was knocked unconscious,' the girl replied in a low voice.

'We do know, however, that there's a renegade band of Snakes rampagin' across this territory. An' we also know the army is seekin' 'em out. I guess it was that band that hit Moose City. Wa'al, s'pose a regiment, or a troop, of soldiers rode into Moose City an' caused the redskins to skeddaddle?' suggested Billy Malone.

'But there ain't no sign of any pursuit,' rasped Rough.

44

'Not yet, though they could appear upon the scene at any moment,' pointed out the 20-year-old.

Two-gun Danny O'Hare scowled darkly. What the youngster said made good sense, and he had no wish to be caught literally with his pants down. Besides, delaying the pleasure to come would surely heighten it. And the thought of tumbling the 17-year-old blonde in the comfort of a soft feather-bed, with a bottle of whiskey to hand for consumption while the others were taking their turn, certainly tickled his fancy. Also, the trading post was situated at Crooked Rock, a mere five miles away. He suddenly grinned and licked his lips in anticipation.

'Trader Tait's it is,' he stated.

'But, Two-gun....!' began Jake Rough.

'The kid's right. There could be soldiers headin' this way,' said O'Hare.

'But, Two-gun...!'

'It ain't a chance I'm willin' to take.'

Jake Rough grimaced. He felt as randy as a polecat and had no wish to wait until they reached Trader Tait's place. However, he knew better than to argue with his friend O'Hare. He shrugged his shoulders resignedly.

'OK,' he grunted. 'Let's git goin'!'

'Miss Lucas can take the Injun's hoss,' said Billy Malone.

Two-gun O'Hare shook his head.

'Nope,' he rasped. 'We dunno how good a rider she is. She might jest try an' make a break for it.'

'But we're armed an'–'

'So, she makes a break for it an' we shoot her. She ain't gonna be no good to us dead, Billy.'

'Guess not, Two-gun.'

'Wa'al, she can ride with you. Reckon that mare of your'n is capable of carryin' the two of yuh?'

'Reckon.' Billy Malone smiled and beckoned to the girl. 'Come on over here, Miss Lucas.'

Rebecca shook her head and slowly backed away. Billy Malone stepped closer,

46

then the girl turned and began to run back down the gorge. She had covered no more than twenty yards when the youngster caught up with her and grasped her by the arm. As he did so, he thrust his face close to hers and whispered into her ear.

'Listen, Miss Lucas,' he hissed. 'I wish you no harm an' I aim to git you outa this. But yuh gotta trust me. Now, for the present, jest play along.'

Thereupon, Billy Malone pulled out his Colt Peacemaker and jabbed it into the girl's ribs.

'Let's have no more strugglin'!' he cried in a loud voice. 'You're comin' with me!'

Rebecca let him drag her towards his two mounted companions. For their benefit, she came haltingly and evidently unwillingly. Her face remained pale and frightened, yet her heart-beat had quickened at the youngster's words. How he proposed to rescue her from his two rough, tough companions, she had no idea. Nevertheless, she felt a sudden surge of hope.

Billy Malone dropped the Colt back into its holster and, while Two-gun O'Hare aimed one of his British Tranters at the blonde, he remounted his chestnut mare. Then, he stretched out his hand towards Rebecca.

'You come on up here or I'll knock yuh senseless,' he rasped.

Rebecca gasped and looked up in horror. Had she been mistaken? Then, he surreptitiously closed his left eye and winked at her. She felt another surge of hope and, without further ado, let him swing her up into the saddle in front of him.

A few moments later, they rode off, with Twogun Danny O'Hare leading, Billy Malone and the girl in the middle, and Jake Rough bringing up the rear. They headed up through the gorge and then branched off northwards, along the trail that led towards Crooked Rock.

Lieutenant Hugh Freeman and his troop of US Cavalry had found it easier than

Low Hill Library
Showell Circus
Low Hill
Wolverhampton
WV10 9JJ
Tel: 01902 556293

Self Service Receipt for Borrowing

Patron: 00226599

Title: Two gun justice
Item: X0000000077067
Due Back: 11/09/2018 23:59

Title: Massacre in Mouse City
Item: X0000000017583
Due Back: 11/09/2018 23:59

Title: leather burners
Item: X0000000149209
Due Back: 11/09/2018 23:59

Title: Broken noose
Item: X0000000057383
Due Back: 11/09/2018 23:59

Title: Stage city
Item: X0000000005907
Due Back: 11/09/2018 23:59

Title: ruthless breed
Item: 07540884561629
Due Back: 11/09/2018 23:59

Total Borrowing: 6
14/08/2018 14:13:15

Thank you for your custom

expected to track Crazy Fox and his band of Snake Indians up into the mountains. They were seven miles from Moose City when they were overtaken by the mayor, Andrew Lucas, and his two companions. The lieutenant had been none too pleased to have civilians riding along, but, once Lucas had explained the reason for their presence, he had felt unable to forbid their doing so.

The abduction of Rebecca Lucas complicated matters, however, and Freeman was still wondering how he might effect the girl's rescue when they reached the point in the trail where Dancing Fox had parted from the rest of the renegade Snakes. It was at this very moment that the Indian's pony chose to trot out from the narrow gorge that opened to the left of the main trail. Lieutenant Freeman immediately held up his hand and brought the troop to a halt. Then he beckoned his sergeant and the three civilians to join him at the head of the column.

'What do you reckon, Sergeant?' he asked.

'Looks like there's been some kinda split, for the main body went thataway,' said McGill, pointing straight ahead.

'Want me to examine the various tracks?' enquired Stone, adding by way of an explanation, 'I was once an Army scout, an' I ain't lost none of my skills.'

Freeman frowned. This was the fellow who had earlier accused the US Army of massacring an Indian village. And now he claimed to have once been an Army scout. The lieutenant had no wish to enlist the man's help, yet he realized that, under the circumstances, he could scarcely refuse.

'OK, Mr ... er...?'

'Stone.'

'Very well, Mr Stone. Examine the tracks an' tell us what you make of 'em.'

Stone dismounted and made a thorough investigation of the hoof-marks on the trail in front of him. Then he set off up the narrow gorge to his left. A couple of minutes later, he returned.

'So, what are your conclusions, Mr Stone?' demanded Freeman.

'Wa'al, Lieutenant,' replied the Kentuckian, 'it seems a single brave broke away an' rode off up into that thar gorge.'

'While the remainder of the band headed straight ahead like the sergeant said?'

'Yessir.' Stone smiled grimly and added, 'There's more.'

'Yes?'

'The Injun's dead.'

'Dead?'

'He's lyin' face down in the dust with a coupla bullet-holes in him.'

'But how...?' began Lucas.

'My guess is he's the brave who abducted your daughter. Reckon he felt he was pretty safe from pursuit an' rode off into that gorge, intending to...' Stone paused, not wishing to spell out what he surmised.

Andrew Lucas paled.

'But – but how come he got hisself shot?' enquired Lew Jackson.

'There are tracks indicatin' there was three

other riders in the gorge. Their hosses were properly shod, so I figure they was white folks.'

'You – you think it was them who shot the Injun?' asked an anxious Andrew Lucas.

'Seems likely.'

'So, why haven't we run into them?' asked Freeman.

'They headed off back up the gorge.'

'Takin' my daughter with them?' cried Lucas.

'That's my guess.'

'But it is only a guess,' said Freeman. 'It's quite possible that she remains with the main body of Snakes. The brave who broke away may have done so for some completely different reason.'

'The lieutenant's right,' growled Sergeant Joe McGill. 'For if, as Mr Stone reckons, those three white folks rescued your daughter, Mr Lucas, why in tarnation would they head back up into the mountains? Surely the obvious thing to do would've been to make for Moose City?'

'Wa'al, Mr Stone?' said Lucas.

'The sergeant has a point. I jest dunno,' said the Kentuckian.

'There's only one way to find out. Follow both trails,' declared Lew Jackson.

'Me and my men, we're heading straight on after Crazy Fox and the main body of Snakes,' stated Lieutenant Freeman firmly.

'Mr Lucas?' enquired Stone.

'I – I figure I'll go along with your supposition. I aim to ride up into that gulch an' follow the tracks of those white folks. However, to succeed in that, I'll need yore services, Mr Stone. Will you ride with me?'

'Yup. I'll ride with you,' said Stone.

'Me, too,' volunteered Lew Jackson.

Lieutenant Hugh Freeman smiled, relieved to be rid of the three civilians.

'That's settled, then,' he remarked cheerfully. 'I wish you good luck, Mr Lucas, and I hope Mr Stone's right about your daughter.'

'Thank you, Lieutenant,' said Lucas.

'Before we split up, though, let me give

you somethin' to ponder on,' said Stone.

'Yes?' replied the subaltern.

'How come it's been so goddam easy to follow Crazy Fox's tracks? Why in blue blazes haven't the Injuns dispersed an' taken separate trails back to their mountain hide-out?'

'What are you getting at?' demanded Freeman.

'I'm suggestin' you could be ridin' into some kinda trap,' said Stone.

'Nonsense!' Freeman shook his head and cried, 'Those stinking, cowardly redskins are fit only to take on unarmed civilians, women and children. They wouldn't dare tackle the army.'

'Wa'al, think about it,' said Stone, as the lieutenant gave the command to ride on.

The Kentuckian watched the soldiers disappear from view, and then he and his two companions turned their horses' heads and set off up into the gorge. They passed the dead body of Dancing Fox and continued to the top of the gorge. There, they

54

turned northwards and, like Two-gun Danny O'Hare and his compadres, proceeded along the trail leading to Crooked Rock.

THREE

Lieutenant Hugh Freeman and his troopers pressed on deeper and deeper into the forest that coated the lower slopes of the Blue Mountains. Considering the difficult terrain through which they were passing, the Indians' tracks remained surprisingly easy to follow.

Presently, they reached a point where the trail emerged from the forest and vanished into a deep ravine. As they approached its rock-strewn entrance, Sergeant Joe McGill rode forward until he was alongside the young officer.

'I've been thinkin', sir,' he growled.

'Oh, yes, Sergeant?'

'Yessir. I – er – I've been thinkin' 'bout what that feller Stone said.' McGill paused, before adding quietly, "bout us ridin' into a trap.'

'You seriously think that cowardly savage, Crazy Fox, would dare attack us?'

'He's certainly a murderous dog, sir. But I ain't so sure he's a coward.'

'You contradicting me, Sergeant?'

'No, sir. Only...'

'Only nothing, Sergeant. We are pursuing Crazy Fox, not Crazy Horse. We are chasing a small band of renegade Snakes, not the entire Sioux nation.' Freeman laughed harshly. 'I think perhaps, Sergeant, you are getting a li'l too old for this life. Mebbe you oughta think about quitting the army.'

McGill scowled darkly. He had been assigned to Hugh Freeman's troop as a seasoned soldier who could counsel and advise the callow young subaltern. But Freeman's arrogance knew no bounds. He was not about to accept advice from his sergeant, however experienced the sergeant might be. McGill promptly shut his mouth and, as the troop advanced into the ravine, dropped back a few paces.

The troop was halfway along the ravine

when the attack began. Perpendicular rock walls lined both sides and, from the tops of these cliffs, the Indians suddenly poured forth a murderous fusillade. A lethal mixture of bullets and arrows rained down upon the hapless soldiers.

Amongst the first to die was the young lieutenant. He was hit in the back and the chest simultaneously, an arrow thudding into the middle of his back and a bullet ripping into his body just beneath the right collar-bone. He toppled from his horse and, as he struggled to get to his feet, a third shot struck him plumb in the centre of his forehead and blasted his brains out of the back of his skull.

In the ensuing few moments, soldier after soldier was toppled from his horse. Scarcely a shot was returned, so sudden, unexpected and merciless was the Snakes' fire. Two who did manage to discharge their carbines were Troopers John Hurley and Vic Moore. They, along with Sergeant Joe McGill, were the only survivors of this, the second massacre to be perpetrated by Crazy Fox and his braves that day. Sunday, usually a day of peace, had, on this occasion, become a day of violent death.

'C'mon! Let's git the hell outa here!' exclaimed McGill

The two troopers needed no second urging. They followed the sergeant at full gallop back down the ravine. A hail of bullets and arrows pursued them and, as they emerged from its narrow environs, John Hurley was nicked in the left upper-arm by a bullet. It was, however, only the slightest of flesh-wounds, no more than a graze, and he continued his gallop through the forest and down the mountainside.

'Goddam the lieutenant for an arrogant lunkhead!' muttered McGill beneath his breath, as he rode at breakneck speed towards the distant plain. Although he could not see them, he knew that Crazy Fox and his band of renegades would surely be in hot pursuit. The vital question was, could he and the two troopers out-ride them?

In their haste, the three soldiers veered off the course they had taken up into the mountains. And, as a result, they found themselves pursuing a parallel trail, which, by chance, took them down through the gorge in which Dancing Fox had met his death.

This proved to be their salvation, for, when Crazy Fox spotted the fallen figure of his brother, he straightaway called a halt to the chase. The Indians reined in their horses and quickly dismounted. The first to kneel down beside the prostrate Snake was Crazy Fox himself. He gently turned his brother over onto his back. Then he let loose a howl of anguish. Grief and rage mingled in his twisted black heart.

'Who has done this?' he cried.

'Could it be the white girl?' asked one of his braves.

'What white girl?' demanded Crazy Fox.

'The one your brother carried off,' replied the brave.

'He carried off a white girl?'

'Yes; that is why he was unable to keep pace with the rest of us.'

Crazy Fox stared in amazement at the brave. He had led the attack upon Moose City and the retreat from the township into the mountains. Consequently, he had not seen Dancing Fox carry off Rebecca Lucas, nor had he realized that his brother was not amongst the braves at his back. So intent was he on luring Lieutenant Hugh Freeman and his troop into a trap that he had closed his mind to everything else. Even when setting up the ambush, he had failed to observe that Dancing Fox was not present.

'There have been several horses here.'

Crazy Fox turned towards the speaker. Greyhaired, wizened and gnome-like beneath his shapeless, wide-brimmed hat and buffalo robe, Fire Lance was, by a good number of years, the oldest in the Snake war-party. He was also by far their best tracker.

'What do you see?' enquired Crazy Fox eagerly.

'They are white men's horses. Six altogether.'

'They must have come upon Dancing Fox and the white girl when he and she...' began another of the braves.

'Enough!' snapped Crazy Fox.

He scowled angrily. He had often warned his brother that his preoccupation with white women would be the death of him. And so it had proved. It had evidently been a chance encounter with the white men, but one that had resulted in Dancing Fox's being shot in the back. Crazy Fox shook his head. His brother had never felt quite the same hatred for the white man as he had. Dancing Fox had ridden with him willingly enough, yet it had not been murder, but rather rape that was in his mind. The white women ravished by Dancing Fox were many. However, he would ravish no more.

'The white men have taken the girl,' said Fire Lance.

'Yes.'

'But I do not think all six ride together.'

'No?'

'No, Crazy Fox. The tracks are quite clear. Three horsemen only rode down the gorge. It is they, I believe, who shot Dancing Fox and took the girl.'

'In which direction?'

'Back up the gorge.'

'And the other three horsemen? What of them?'

'Again the tracks are clear. They were with the bluecoats.'

'You are certain, Fire Lance?'

'I am. They detached themselves from the main body and rode into the mouth of the gorge.'

'But why should they do that?'

'Dancing Fox's pony, it is gone. Perhaps it wandered out of the gorge and was spotted by the bluecoats?'

'These three, then, are soldiers?'

'I assume so, Crazy Fox.'

'Hmm.'

'These three soldiers, they pursued the other three up the gorge. That is my reading of the tracks.'

'But why?'

'If they knew Dancing Fox had taken the white girl, perhaps they went in search of her?'

'But she is again in the hands of her own people!'

'Men who did not, as might have been expected, continue down the mountain and head for Moose City.'

'Yes, that is strange, is it not?' mused Crazy Fox. He turned to two of his braves. 'You will take my brother to our camp and prepare him for his funeral,' he decreed.

The pair looked less than happy at this prospect, but they knew better than to argue with Crazy Fox.

'And the rest of us, do we recommence our pursuit of the bluecoat sergeant and his two companions?' enquired Fire Lance.

'No,' said Crazy Fox. 'We give chase to my brother's killers. And, when we catch them, they shall die the death of a thousand cuts.'

So saying, the renegade leader leapt into

the saddle and, seconds later, the Snake Indians were galloping up the gorge in the direction taken by, firstly, Two-gun Danny O'Hare and his compadres and, secondly, Andrew Lucas, Lew Jackson and the Kentuckian.

The band's departure was witnessed with interest by Sergeant Joe McGill. As soon as he and the two troopers had exited through the mouth of the gorge, he had instructed them to ride hell-for-leather to Fort Franklin and report what had happened.

'Ain't you comin' with us, Sarge?' Vic Moore had asked.

'Nope,' McGill had informed him. 'I aim to see what occurs when them goddam savages come across the body of that thar' dead Injun.'

The other two had protested, but McGill had remained obdurate, and, so, still protesting, they had recommenced their ride westward. McGill meantime, had hidden his horse in a clump of cottonwoods and made his way up a zigzag path to the rim of the gorge.

Now, from this vantage point, he was able to see and hear all that was happening below on the floor of the gorge. Not that he understood a word that was spoken, for he had no knowledge of the Snake tongue. However, it was clear that Crazy Fox and his followers intended to pursue the killers of the dead Snake Indian. Perhaps, McGill pondered, their preoccupation with hunting down those killers might make them careless, less concerned with the possibility that they, too, could be pursued.

The sergeant waited until the last Snake had vanished round a bend in the gorge, and then he began hurriedly to descend the zigzag path. Once he had regained the cottonwoods, he unhitched his horse and straightaway set off in the wake of the two surviving troopers.

FOUR

It was late afternoon when Two-gun Danny O'Hare and his companions reached the small trading post at Crooked Rock. It consisted of a large two-storey cabin, with a sign over the door proclaiming the cabin to be 'Trader Tait's'; half-a-dozen smaller one-storey cabins belonging to various trappers; and a small corral in which grazed some rather run-down-looking cayuses and several mules.

The three riders dismounted, Billy Malone taking advantage of the fact that his horse momentarily blocked the others' view, to again whisper into Rebecca's ear.

'Now, Miss Lucas, when we git inside, you continue to struggle an' make a fuss,' he hissed, adding, 'I'll play along, but, don't worry, I intend gittin' yuh outa this.' Aloud, he snapped, 'C'mon, quit wrigglin' or I'm liable to smash your face in!'

'Hell, don't do that, Billy!' cried O'Hare. 'We don't wanta mess up her pretty face none.'

'No?'

'Nope; that wouldn't do at all. I like 'em pretty.'

'Me, too,' averred Jake Rough, licking his lips and leering lasciviously at the 17-year-old blonde.

'Why don't you jest take me back to Moose City?' cried Rebecca. 'Pa, he'll reward yuh real well.'

'I don't doubt it, Miss,' said O'Hare. 'But the reward'll be the same whether or not we have some sport with you. An' I sure do fancy a tumble. Whaddya say, Jake?'

'Yes, sirree!' exclaimed a lustful Jake Rough.

'Wa'al, let's go inside,' cried Billy Malone.

'See, Miss, you've gone an' got the kid all steamed up, too!' laughed O'Hare.

'But–' Rebecca began to protest.

'Shuddup!' snapped Billy Malone, and he pushed her through the doorway and into Trader Tait's emporium.

The cabin was part general store and part bar-room. Trader Tait bought furs from the trappers and, in turn, sold them everything they might need: weapons, ammunition, clothing, provisions, whiskey, tobacco and various other incidentals. He was a shrewd, 45-year-old Scot, slimly built and of medium height, with intelligent brown eyes and dark brown hair streaked with grey. He wore a neatly pressed white shirt and smart black trousers, over which he had tied a dark green apron.

As the three men and the girl entered, Trader Tait was in the act of replenishing the glasses of two buffalo hunters, who were propped against the bar counter. Seated at a few tables scattered across the bar-room were several trappers. All looked up with interest at the new arrivals.

In accordance with Billy Malone's instructions, Rebecca continued to struggle and protest. She turned her lovely blue eyes towards Trader Tait and the two buffalo hunters.

'Please!' she cried. 'Won't you help me?'

'Er ... in what way, Miss?' enquired Tait.

'These men, they...'

'We saved her from a Snake Injun. He was gonna rape an', in all likelihood, kill her,' interjected O'Hare.

'Is that right?' Tait asked the girl.

'Y-yes. But–'

'But nuthin'. You'd be dead but for us,' declared Rough.

'An' we're simply lookin' for our just rewards,' grinned O'Hare.

'Oh, aye?' said Tait.

'Yeah. We jest want ourselves a li'l fun. Hell, surely a man's entitled to some sport?' remarked O'Hare.

'They – they're proposin' to – to rape me!' cried Rebecca, struggling helplessly in Billy Malone's firm grip.

'Are ye aimin' tae rape her?' enquired Tait.

'Rape's a nasty word,' hissed O'Hare.

'It's no' exactly a nice thing tae dae,' retorted the Scot.

'Like I said, we're jest claimin' our reward,' said O'Hare. He smiled menacingly at the trader and continued, 'Does that bother you any?'

Trader Tait eyed the trio nervously. Billy Malone didn't worry him unduly, but the other two certainly scared him. He observed Danny O'Hare's hands hovering above the pearl handles of his two British Tranters. The man was, without question, a professional gunslinger. And he had no doubt that O'Hare's scar-faced companion was also a shootist. To provoke either would be to invite sudden and certain death.

He glanced round the bar-room. He knew most of his customers pretty well. All were fairly rough and ready, but none was capable of out-drawing and out-shooting a professional gunfighter. It was evident from the looks on their faces that they felt a measure of sympathy towards the innocent young girl. They had all, in their time, used and misused sporting women, but they drew the line at violating someone of Rebecca's tender years and ingenuousness. Nevertheless, it was equally evident that none was prepared to take a stand against O'Hare and his companions.

'No,' the trader lied unhappily. 'It doesnae bother me.'

'Good!' O'Hare grinned broadly. 'Then, you won't object to rentin' us a room for the night?'

'I'm no' sure we have a room free at the moment.'

'Yo're tellin' me they're all taken?'

'Well ... er...'

'We know you got rooms upstairs which yuh rent out to folks passin' through,' growled Jake Rough.

'So, jest how many of 'em *have* you got occupied?' enquired O'Hare.

'I'm no' exactly sure, but–'

'None, I reckon,' rasped Rough.

'It's no' that they're a' taken. It's simply that they're not prepared.'

'There's a bed in each, I s'pose?' said O'Hare.

'Er ... yes.'

'That's all we need. One bed.'

The two gunslingers laughed harshly, while what little colour was left drained from Rebecca's face and she gazed imploringly at the trader.

'No!' she cried. 'You cain't–'

'Shuddup!' snapped Billy Malone.

'That's right; be quiet,' hissed O'Hare and, turning to Trader Tait, he demanded 'Wa'al, whaddya say?'

Tait looked distinctly ill at ease. He had no wish to become a party to the rape of the young girl, yet he dared not refuse the shootist.

'OK,' he muttered, and then, in an attempt to delay matters, asked, 'Will ye no' be wantin' a drink first?'

O'Hare glanced quizzically at his scar-faced companion.

'Yeah, why not?' said Rough.

'Two whiskies,' snapped O'Hare.

As they stepped up to the bar, so the two buffalo hunters threw back their beers and slammed down their glasses onto the counter.

'Be seein' yuh, Trader,' said the taller of the two.

'You fellers ain't leavin' on account of us, are yuh?' enquired O'Hare, fixing the buffalo hunters with a venomous eye.

'That wouldn't be very friendly,' added Rough darkly.

'We – we don't wanta cause no – no offence,' stammered the second hunter. 'It – it's jest that we gotta be on our way.'

'That's right,' declared the taller one.

'Wa'al, before yuh go, mebbe you'd like to pay for the drinks my friend ordered?' suggested Rough.

The buffalo hunters exchanged nervous looks. They were no cowards and they had their self-respect to consider. On the other hand, they knew they could never hope to out-gun the two shootists. Pride struggled against discretion. The others in the bar-room held their breath as the tension mounted.

It was at this moment that Billy Malone chose to act. Both gunmen had their backs to him and the girl. He might never get a better chance. Swiftly, he drew the Colt Peacemaker from his holster, reversed the gun and, holding it by the barrel, aimed and struck two sharp blows. His first hit Two-gun Danny O'Hare plumb on the back of the skull, while the second hit Jake Rough on a similar spot. Both men grunted and pitched face downwards onto the bar-room floor.

There followed a stunned silence, broken eventually by the taller of the two buffalo hunters.

'Holy cow!' he exclaimed. 'You sure gave each of them no-account bastards one helluva thump!'

'That's right,' averred Trader Tait, leaning over the bar-counter and eyeing the pros-trate gunmen. 'They're both oot cold.'

'Yeah. Wa'al, me an' Miss Lucas, we plan

77

to lam outa here.' Billy Malone now held the revolver by the butt, with his finger on the trigger. 'I hope none of you folks is gonna object?' he added quietly.

'Er ... no; you an' the young lady are free tae leave whenever ye like,' said Tait.

'Thanks. An' I'd 'preciate it if'n' when the two sleepin' beauties come to, you don't tell 'em which direction we took.'

'Don't worry, kid,' smiled the trader. 'We're no' gonna tell 'em nuthin'.'

He and the others watched Billy Malone and the girl hurry from the cabin. Nobody moved to prevent their escape. Indeed, all of them were relieved that their failure to intervene had not resulted in the girl's rape at the hands of the two shootists.

Outside, Billy Malone turned to Rebecca.

'Can you ride a hoss?' he enquired anxiously.

'Yes, I sure can,' replied Rebecca.

'Good! Then, you take my mare. She's pretty darned quiet. I'll ride Two-gun's stallion. He's a mite frisky.'

'Right.'

As they mounted, Billy Malone turned his horse's head towards the north.

'Wa'al, let's git goin',' he said.

'But – but you're headin' on north! Ain't we goin' back the way we came?' demanded the girl.

'Nope,' he said.

'But–'

'When those two sonsofbitches recover their senses, they're gonna come lookin' for us.'

'I s'pose.'

'No question. An' it's a long ways 'tween here an' Moose City.'

'Yes.'

'So, they could mebbe catch us up.'

Rebecca shuddered at the thought.

'I guess they could at that,' she murmured nervously.

'Wa'al, they'll almost certainly expect us to head back the way we jest came,' said Billy Malone. 'Which is why we're gonna ride in the opposite direction. OK, it'll mean we have a longer journey, but that'll surely be worthwhile if'n' we succeed in throwin' Two-gun an' Jake off our tracks?'

Rebecca nodded.

'How far north are yuh proposin' we ride?' she asked.

'Oh, a fair way! As far as Freedom Falls,' said Billy Malone. 'Then we'll turn westward an' continue on till we hit the John Day. We'll cross the river at Jingle's Ferry an', from there, we simply follow the trail south to Moose City.'

Rebecca smiled approvingly. Her young rescuer's plan seemed to make good sense. Twogun Danny O'Hare and Jake Rough would surely never expect them to ride northwards.

'To the north it is, then!' she cried, and she promptly set off at a gallop.

Billy Malone grinned, dug his heels into the flanks of Two-gun Danny O'Hare's stallion and rode off in hot pursuit.

Meantime, inside the trading post, the two gunmen were slowly recovering. They staggered groggily to their feet. Both had splitting headaches and felt as though the bar-room were spinning round and round. They were also in the foulest of tempers.

'Bring us them goddam whiskies,' gasped O'Hare.

Trader Tait hesitated. He felt like telling O'Hare to go to the Devil. But he decided that discretion was indeed the better part of valour. Even half-stunned, the gunman remained a dangerous fellow to cross.

O'Hare and Rough collapsed onto chairs at the nearest table and, resting their heads in their hands, groaned and shut their eyes. They stayed in this position for some minutes, not stirring even when Trader Tait placed the two glasses of whiskey on the table in front of them.

Eventually, they sat up and began to slowly drink the red-eye. Two-gun Danny O'Hare turned his baleful gaze upon his host.

'It was the kid KO'd us, wasn't it?' he demanded of Trader Tait.

'Aye. He gave ye both a good bashin',' commented Tait.

The buffalo hunters chuckled, as did the others in the bar-room. All had been highly delighted when Billy Malone administered the *coup de grâce*.

'You let him an' the girl high-tail it outa here?' snarled Jake Rough.

'Yup. We figured it wasn't none of our business,' stated the taller buffalo hunter.

''Sright,' agreed his partner.

'Wa'al, let's git after 'em,' rasped O'Hare, hurriedly throwing back the remains of his drink.

Jake Rough promptly followed suit, and the two shootists staggered outside, where they discovered that O'Hare's stallion was nowhere to be seen.

'Goddammit!' he roared. 'That young sonofabitch has stolen my hoss!'

'So, what in tarnation do we do?' cried Rough, as he clumsily mounted his sorrel. 'You gonna climb up behind me?'

'If'n' I do that, there ain't no way we're

gonna catch Billy an' the girl,' retorted
O'Hare.

'Guess not.'

'We need another hoss.'

'Wa'al, there's some hosses in that thar
corral.'

'Broken-down, knock-kneed cayuses,
most of em.'

'It's one of them or nuthin', Two-gun.'

'Yeah, Jake, I know it.' O'Hare turned to
find that all of Trader Tait's customers had
followed them out of the cabin. Trader Tait
himself stood in the doorway, with a loaded
shotgun aimed at the two shootists. 'Why
the hell are you pointin' that goddam gun at
us?' he demanded angrily.

'I look upon it as a kind of insurance,'
replied Tait.

'Insurance?'

'You are gonna want tae buy a horse off
me, is that no' the case?'

'Yeah.'

'Weel, I want payin' in dollars, no' in
bullets.'

Tait smiled. However fast on the draw the two gunslingers might be, he reckoned they would be hard put to it in present circumstances to out-gun him, considering the shotgun was cocked on both hammers and all he had to do was squeeze the trigger.

O'Hare scowled. He was half-inclined to call Trader Tait's bluff, but he observed, out of the corner of his eye, that the two buffalo hunters had pulled their rifles from their saddle-boots and that a number of the trappers were fingering the butts of their revolvers.

'How much?' he growled.

'One hundred dollars,' replied Tait coolly.

'One hundred dollars!'

'That's daylight robbery!' cried Rough.

Sure is,' agreed Tait, with a grin, 'but that's the price. Take it or leave it.'

'Holy cow!'

'Ye can take your choice of a' the horses in yon corral. An', oot o' the generosity o' my he'rt, I'll throw in a saddle.'

'You – you...'

'Weel?'

O'Hare glared at the trader, but he knew he was beaten. He had to have a horse. Reluctantly, he dug deep inside his knee-length black coat and pulled out a roll of ten-dollar bills, the remains of his and Rough's last bank job. He slowly counted out ten and offered them to Tait.

Tait smiled, but did not lower the shotgun.

'Gie the money tae Sammy there,' he said, indicating one of the trappers, a friend of several years' standing.

O'Hare did as he was bid and, with Tait's and several other guns still trained upon him, he went about the business of choosing a horse and saddling it. He selected the best of a bad bunch, a gangly-looking pinto. Then, when he was finally mounted, the gunman turned to face Tait.

'You – you'll pay dearly for this!' he snarled. 'One day I'll settle this score!'

'I dinna think so,' replied Tait. 'For, if either of ye ever return tae Crooked Rock, me an' my friends, we'll shoot on sight.'

'That's a promise,' added one of the trappers, emboldened by the situation in which he found himself

Two-gun Danny O'Hare glared at each man in turn, but said nothing more. Instead, he simply turned his horse's head and, with Jake Rough following, set off at as furious a pace as he could muster.

The two gunslingers naturally assumed that Billy Malone and the girl had returned whence they came. In consequence, they rode southwards, in quite the opposite direction to that taken by their quarry.

FIVE

Two-gun Danny O'Hare and Jake Rough were three miles along the trail when they ran into Andrew Lucas, Deputy Marshal Lew Jackson and the Kentuckian, Jack Stone, on their way towards Crooked Rock.

The mayor of Moose City held up his hand, gesturing the two gunmen to halt. O'Hare, anxious to catch up with his quarry, felt disinclined to do so and would have ridden on had he not encountered the grim gaze of the Kentuckian. Something in Stone's eye told him that he had better pause and, consequently, he reined in his pinto. An equally impatient Jake Rough reluctantly pulled up beside him.

'You fellers want somethin'?' enquired O'Hare gruffly.

'Yeah,' said Lucas. 'We're lookin' for three men an' a 17-year-old girl.'

'The girl's blonde an' pretty, an' she'll be ridin' the same hoss as one of the men, for they've only got three hosses between them,' added Lew Jackson.

O'Hare eyed the badge pinned to the breast pocket of the young deputy's ill-fitting brown jacket, the sight of which made the shootist feel distinctly uneasy.

'The girl is my daughter,' stated Lucas. 'An' we fear for her safety. We believe that three unknown horsemen came across her an' the Injun she was with, an' rescued her from the Injun. But, for some reason, they haven't headed back towards Moose City.'

'You – you sure 'bout all this?' enquired O'Hare.

'Yeah. We know the Injun abducted her,' remarked Stone.

'An' we found him shot dead a ways back,' said Lew Jackson. 'Mr Stone here deduced that there was three riders from the tracks we found near the dead body.'

'Oh, yeah? You some kinda tracker, Mr ... er ... Stone?' rasped O'Hare.

'Yup. I was once an Army scout, an' I was taught the tricks of the trade by a Kiowa named Red Cloud,' said Stone.

'So, have yuh seen 'em?' demanded Lucas anxiously.

O'Hare shook his head.

'Nope, cain't say we have,' he replied. 'Have we, Jake?'

'No, Two-gun. They certainly ain't passed this way,' confirmed Rough.

'I see.' Andrew Lucas's face dropped. 'Wa'al, thanks, anyway,' he said quietly.

'Sorry, mister. I sure hope you find your daughter,' said O'Hare.

'Yeah. Mebbe the fellers who rescued her from the Injun are jest takin' a kinda round-about route back to Moose City?' suggested Rough.

'Mebbe.'

'Good day, then, gents.'

'So long.'

Andrew Lucas watched the two men ride

past. To say that he was disappointed they had not seen Rebecca and her three rescuers, would be to put it mildly.

As for Two-gun Danny O'Hare and Jake Rough, they continued to follow the trail southwards. But they were as dismayed as Andrew Lucas.

'Goddammit!' snarled O'Hare. 'If'n' Billy an' the girl had headed back the way we came, they'd've ridden slap bang into her father an' his pals.'

'Guess so.'

'So, whaddya reckon, Jake?'

'I reckon they rode north.'

'But Moose City lies to the south-west.'

'Which is why they rode north, Two-gun. To throw us off their trail. Billy Malone ain't no fool, y'know.'

'The cunnin' li'l sonofabitch!'

'So, what now, Two-gun?'

'Let me think.' O'Hare pondered on the situation for some moments. Then, at last, he said, 'I figure Billy's plan must be to head a ways north along the trail, an' then turn westward an' drop down outa the mountains.'

'That'll take 'em eventually to the John Day.'

'Which they'll need to cross.'

'They could ford the river easy enough at several places south of here. But up north'

'They'll most likely aim for Jingle's Ferry.'

'If we leave this here trail an' strike off northwestward...'

'We might well reach Jingle's Ferry ahead of 'em.' O'Hare smiled grimly. 'Billy Malone's gonna pay for his treachery with his life, an', as for the girl...'

The tall, rake-thin gunslinger did not complete his sentence, but his companion guessed, from his lascivious leer, what he had in mind for the young girl. Jake Rough grinned.

'Let's git goin', then,' he snarled.

The two riders wheeled their horses round and began their cross-country descent of the mountains. They had some pretty tough terrain to negotiate, and they had no time to lose, if they were to reach Jingle's Ferry in time to prevent Billy Malone and Rebecca Lucas from crossing the John Day. Once on the other side, a short ride would take them to the safety of Moose City.

Andrew Lucas and his two companions, meantime, continued to ride northwards towards Crooked Rock. As they rode, they discussed their encounter with Danny O'Hare and Jake Rough.

'Whaddya make of them two fellers?' enquired Lucas.

'I didn't like the look of 'em one li'l bit,' said Lew Jackson. 'A coupla no-account critters. What's yore opinion, Mr Stone?'

'I agree with you, Lew. My guess is, they're on the wrong side of the law. But, Hell, that don't mean they was lyin' to us!' said Stone.

'No. After all, why should they?' remarked Lucas.

'Wa'al, if they ain't seen Rebecca an' her three rescuers, does that mean we're on the wrong trail?' enquired the young deputy marshal.

'Mebbe. Mebbe not,' said Stone.

'So, do we keep headin' north?' asked Lew Jackson.

'For the moment, yes. There's a tradin' post another mile or so up the trail,' said Lucas. 'I figure we can make some enquiries there. Then we'll decide on our next move.'

'Yeah, that makes sense,' agreed the Kentuckian.

The young deputy marshal nodded, and they proceeded on their way northwards.

It did not take them long to reach Crooked Rock, where, upon entering the bar-room-cum-general-store, they found Trader Tait and his customers still discussing the events that had taken place there earlier that afternoon.

As Andrew Lucas ordered beers for himself and his two companions, the three quietly waited and listened to the conversation. This had neither slackened nor ceased upon their arrival, but had continued unabated. When, presently, the mayor felt he had heard enough, he intervened.

'Excuse me,' he said, 'but the girl you are talkin' about happens to be my daughter.'

This remark occasioned all talk to abruptly terminate. A short silence followed, which was eventually broken by Trader Tait.

'Trader Tait at your service,' said the Scot genially. 'An' you'll be...?'

'Andrew Lucas, mayor of Moose City,' replied Lucas. 'An' these here are deppity marshal, Lew Jackson, an' the famous Kentuckian gunfighter, Jack Stone.'

'Pleased tae meet ye, gents.'

'From what you were sayin', I gather my daughter rode off with the youngest of her three companions?'

'Aye.'

'The other two had intended to ... er...'

'Rape her, Mr Lucas. They seemed tae think this was a fair reward for havin' saved her frae the clutches o' her Injun captor.'

'But their young friend did not agree?'

'It would seem not. He laid the pair o' them low an' then he an' your daughter high-tailed it outa here.'

'Those two fellers we encountered back there on the trail, they must've been her would-be rapists,' commented Lew Jackson.

'Describe them,' said Tait.

'A tall, thin feller in a black coat an' stovepipe hat, an' a big, brawny, bearded galoot with a livid white scar disfigurin' his forehead,' replied the youngster.

'That's them!' exclaimed the trapper named Sammy.

'So it is,' confirmed Tait.

'Guess they figured that the youngster an' your daughter was headed south,' said the taller buffalo hunter.

'But they figured wrong,' said Stone.

'Yeah.'

'Yup. If'n' the kid an' Rebecca had headed south, they'd have surely run into us?'

'Guess so.'

'Did anyone here observe in which direction they fled?' asked Lucas.

Tait and the others all shook their heads. None had followed the pair outdoors. They had been too preoccupied with the two stunned shootists.

'So, all we know for sure is that the kid an' Rebecca didn't head south,' stated the mayor. 'Which, I guess, leaves us with several other options. East or west. North. Or...'

'Most likely they would've ridden northwards along the trail, then dropped doon outa the mountains, aimin' for Jingle's Ferry,' said Trader Tait. 'They would want tae cross the river, I suppose?'

'Yes.'

'Weel, that's the nearest point north of here where they'd be able tae get across.'

'The shortest an' quickest route to Jingle's Ferry would surely be to strike north-west from here?' said Lucas.

'Mebbe. But that's pretty darned wild country. A man could git hisself lost cuttin' across it. The safer, easier route to follow is the trail north to jest below Freedom Falls. There's a fork in the trail there that leads down through the mountains an' straight to

Jingle's Ferry,' said the trapper called Sammy.

Andrew Lucas considered this proposition. Would Rebecca's young rescuer have taken the safer option? There was absolutely no way of telling.

'I suggest we split up,' he said finally. 'Two of us continue northwards along the trail, while the other cuts across country.'

'That seems sensible,' growled Stone. 'You an' the deppity head north. I'll take the north-westerly route.'

'Are you sure, Mr Stone? Like the trapper said, you could easily git yoreself lost. Mebbe I should take—'

'No. You stick to the trail with the deppity. That's the most likely option. I'll wait for you at Jingle's Ferry,' said the Kentuckian.

And so it was settled. The three men finished their beers and took their leave of Trader Tait and the others.

By the time they emerged from the cabin, dusk was fast descending. They quickly mounted and, skirting the corral, rode away from the small settlement of Crooked Rock. All three halted for a moment beside the trail.

'Good luck!' cried the Kentuckian.

'Same to you, Mr Stone,' responded Lucas.

Thereupon, he and Lew Jackson galloped off along the trail, while Stone began his descent through the forest and down the mountain.

SIX

Darkness had long since fallen, but still Billy Malone and the girl pressed on. Rebecca was desperately tired. However, her fear of being overtaken by Two-gun Danny O'Hare and Jake Rough far exceeded her weariness. And so, although almost asleep in the saddle, the 17-year-old gamely kept going.

Billy Malone realized that Rebecca was nearly at the end of her tether and that a rest was necessary. He hoped he had thrown his erstwhile compadres off their trail. If so, a break in their journey would be sensible. If not...

The youngster shuddered at the thought. As he did so, they rounded a bend and, ahead of them, spied Freedom Falls. The water cascaded down the mountainside.

Billy Malone peered upwards to the top of the waterfall. A narrow track zigzagged up the mountain beside the fall. At its summit was a flat hilltop strewn with enormous boulders. The perfect hideaway. The horses could be safely hidden amongst the boulders, and he would command an excellent view of the trail. From that eminence, the youngster would be able to see anyone approaching several miles away. At least, he could do so in daylight hours. But, then, while it remained dark, they should be safe anyway.

'OK,' he said, 'we're gonna stop awhile.'

'No,' said Rebecca wearily, 'we cain't. If we do, those two villains will catch us up. An' then—'

'There's a good hideaway up ahead,' Billy Malone interrupted her. 'An', if'n' we don't stop soon, you're gonna plumb drop outa that saddle.'

Rebecca sighed. She knew what he said was true, yet she was terrified that they might be caught.

'I tell you, we – we cain't stop. Those men–'

'Ain't gonna find us. An', even if they do, there's no chance they'll git to us. I tell yuh, Miss Lucas, the place I've got in mind is a sight easier to defend than even Fort Franklin itself. Those sonsofbitches come within a hundred yards an' I'll blast their goddam brains out.'

'Wa'al, if you're sure,' Rebecca murmured.

She was almost dead in the saddle. To lie down and sleep would be sheer bliss. The girl was so very, very tired. She dearly wanted to believe him.

'I'm sure,' said Billy Malone confidently.

'OK,' said the girl.

The youngster smiled and proceeded to lead Rebecca slowly up the narrow path that wound its way to the hilltop above Freedom Falls. Once upon the summit, they dismounted and unsaddled their horses, which Billy Malone then began to hobble. This task completed, he drew Rebecca over to

101

one of the large boulders overlooking the waterfall. She peered out into the darkness.

'You – you cain't see nobody out there!' she exclaimed.

'Wa'al, nobody out there can see us either,' retorted Billy Malone. 'An', believe me, Miss Lucas, should Two-gun an' Jake try clamberin' up the path we jest climbed, I'll hear 'em for sure.'

'Yes, I s'pose so.'

''Course. An', in the mornin', we'll command one helluva view. Nobody'll be able to git within several miles of Freedom Falls without us spottin' 'em.'

'Freedom Falls? So, that's what the waterfall beneath us is called! Ain't this where you said we turn due west an' head on down the mountains towards Jingle's Ferry?'

'That's right, Miss Lucas.'

'You know, you don't have to keep callin' me Miss Lucas. Rebecca will do jest fine,' said the girl.

'Thanks, Miss ... er ... Rebecca,' said her young protector. 'I'd like that.'

Rebecca nodded wearily.

'OK, Billy, what now?' she asked.

'You git yourself a few hours' sleep. Yo're plain tuckered out.'

'But–'

'No buts, Rebecca. If you're aimin' to complete the ride to Jingle's Ferry, you're gonna need some rest.'

'I'm still scared that Mr O'Hare an' Mr Rough will catch up with us.'

'Don't be. I figure, by headin' north, we threw 'em clean off our tracks.' Billy Malone gave the girl's shoulder a reassuring pat and added, 'Anyways, I'll keep a good watch.'

'But aren't you tired, too, Billy?'

'Me? Hell, no!' lied the youngster. 'I reckon I could ride forty-eight hours or more 'fore I'd feel the least bit tired.'

Rebecca took the youngster's blanket roll and wrapped it round her. Then, resting her head against her saddle, she almost immediately dropped into a deep sleep.

He, meantime, took up a position which commanded an excellent view of the trail and there began his watch. However, his boast that he was not the least bit tired soon proved to be a hollow one. Even the pangs of hunger which he felt were insufficient to keep him awake. Although he struggled manfully to maintain his vigil, Billy Malone found himself continually nodding off. He staved off sleep for an hour or more, but eventually he succumbed and, slumping down behind the boulder on which he had rested his Winchester, he, too, fell into a deep sleep.

Dawn was breaking when Billy Malone presently awoke. But it was not the rising of the sun that had woken him. Rather it was the cold muzzle of a Colt Peacemaker pressed against his left temple.

He looked up with a start into the cool blue eyes of Deputy Marshal Lew Jackson.

'Hey, whaddya think yo're doin'?' gasped Billy Malone, looking askance at the badge pinned to Lew Jackson's jacket pocket.

At that same moment, Rebecca awoke to find her father kneeling down beside her.

'Pa!' she cried delightedly.

'Oh, Rebecca, my darlin' daughter!' responded the mayor. And, with tears of relief in his eyes, he asked anxiously, 'What did those sonsofbitches do to you, my dearest?'

'Nuthin', Pa. Not a thing,' said Rebecca, adding, with a smile, 'thanks to Billy here. He saved me.'

'Yeah, so we heard,' acknowledged Lew Jackson.

'Then, mebbe, you'll stop pressin' that gun into my head?' said Billy Malone.

'Sorry.' Lew Jackson withdrew the revolver. 'I jest wanted to be sure you hadn't rescued Miss Lucas for some nefarious purpose of your own,' he remarked.

'Nope. Rapin' young ladies an' holdin' 'em to ransom ain't my style,' stated Billy Malone.

'Then, what is your style?'

'Yes, Mr ... er...?'

'Malone. Billy Malone.'

'Wa'al, as you'll have gathered, I'm

Rebecca's father. Andrew Lucas, mayor of Moose City, at your service. An' this here's our depitty marshal, Lew Jackson.' Lucas smiled broadly and extended his hand. 'So, Mr Malone, jest what is your style?'

'We're interested because of the company yuh chose to keep,' explained Lew Jackson. 'We met up with yore erstwhile companions an' they struck me as a coupla no-account critters.'

'Oh, they sure are, Deppity! They're a coupla outlaws, wanted for several bank robberies an' at least one stagecoach hold-up. You've almost certainly got some "Wanted" posters on 'em. Twogun Danny O'Hare an' Jake Rough.'

'Holy cow!'

'You've heard of 'em, Lew?' enquired Lucas.

'Yup. They ain't only wanted for robbery. They're also wanted for murder in several states.'

'Gosh, Billy!' exclaimed Rebecca. 'How in tarnation did you git yoreself tied up with such men?'

'It's a long story,' said Billy Malone.

'Wa'al, we ain't in no partickler hurry,' commented Lew Jackson.

'Lew's right. Spit it out, Billy,' said Lucas, following his daughter's example and addressing her young rescuer by his given name.

Billy Malone nodded and began haltingly, 'It ... er ... it all began a few months back. In the Wildcat Saloon, in Tuscarora, Nevada.'

'But you don't hail from Nevada?' said Lucas perceptively.

'Nope. I'm a Texan. I'd been on a cattle drive an' was headin' back south, together with the trail boss an' several other cowhands. We stopped off in Tuscarora to have ourselves a li'l fun. A mistake, as it turned out.'

'Yeah?' said Lew Jackson.

'Yeah. We was all enjoyin' ourselves, drinkin' an' chattin' with the saloon girls when a big, fat, red-faced feller in city-style duds stepped in through the Wildcat's doors. He pushed his way through the crowd, knockin' folks aside an' not carin' a damn whether he made 'em spill their beer.'

'Didn't anyone object?' enquired the young deputy.

'Nope. At least, not until he nudged the arm of my trail boss, Greg Somers. Mr Somers, he wasn't none too pleased an' said so in no uncertain terms.' Billy Malone glanced at Rebecca and remarked, 'I don't think I oughta repeat what he said.'

'No, perhaps not,' said Andrew Lucas, with a grin.

'Anyways, the fat feller stepped back a pace. I don't think he'd expected anyone to stand up to him. That's when I intervened. Guess I should've left it to Mr Somers, but I didn't. I planted myself slap bang in front of him an' told him he owed Mr Somers an apology an', while he was at it, he could buy Mr Somers an' the rest of us cowboys some beers.'

'An' what did he say to that?' enquired Lew Jackson.

108

'Nuthin'. The sonofabitch simply gave me a shove an', as I staggered backwards, he went for his gun. He had it out an' aimed at me 'fore I could recover. Then he spoke.' Billy Malone smiled wryly and continued, 'He said he wasn't havin' no goddam kid talkin' to him like that, an' he was gonna teach me a lesson by makin' me do some dancin'.'

'What was he then, the town bully?' asked the mayor.

'Yup. So I found out afterwards. He liked pushin' folks around. An' there was nobody in town prepared to stand up to him. Not jest 'cause he was a vicious, ill-tempered kinda critter. There was another reason, but I'll come to that in a minute. For the moment, there I was, starin' down the barrel of his Colt .45, while he ordered me to untie my gunbelt an' toss my Peacemaker onto the floor.'

'Oh, my gosh!' exclaimed Rebecca.

'Yeah. Wa'al, at my back was the bar-counter, an' directly behind me stood an old brass spittoon. I untied the gunbelt with one hand. Then, as I tossed it an' my gun onto the floor, I grabbed the spittoon with my other hand an' hurled it at the fat feller. This move took him completely by surprise. The spittoon struck him in the chest an' caused him to totter back a yard or so. Before he could recover, I ducked down an' made a grab for my Peacemaker. I guess we fired simultaneously, but, whereas the fat feller missed, I managed to hit him in the shoulder. He never succeeded in loosin' off a second shot. But I did.'

'You killed him, right?' surmised the deputy marshal.

'Right. The slug exploded plumb in the middle of the bastard's forehead an' killed him outright.'

'It was a fair fight, though, an' one which was forced upon you,' commented Lucas.

'In a way.'

'So, what happened next?' demanded the mayor.

'Wa'al, nobody seemed partickerly put out

that I'd shot the fat feller. Quite the reverse. It appeared, as I said earlier, that he was the town bully an' was hated by one an' all. Most folks had been afraid of him, an' even the few who weren't had been disinclined to tangle with him.'

'For another reason, you claimed,' said Rebecca.

'Yeah. The dead man was one Donald Galbraith, younger brother of Tuscarora's sheriff. An' Sheriff Bernie Galbraith was, an' still is, the roughest, toughest peace officer in the entire State of Nevada. A hard, hard man.'

'Ah!'

'I was told this by several people, one of whom was the saloon-keeper,' said Billy Malone. 'He advised me to lam outa town pronto. Otherwise, he reckoned, the sheriff would undoubtedly arrest me for murder, an' I'd hang for sure.'

'But – but it – it wasn't murder!' exclaimed Rebecca.

'I know.'

'Surely, then, all those who witnessed the gunfight–' she began.

'Would testify on my behalf?'

'Yes.'

'Nope. They'd say what Sheriff Galbraith told 'em to say. At least, that was the saloon-keeper's opinion.'

'What about the trail boss an' the rest of your cowboy pals?'

'The saloon-keeper reckoned the sheriff'd be certain to run 'em outa town before my trial took place.'

'I see. So, you took the saloon-keeper's advice an' lammed outa town?'

'Yup. Mr Somers figured it'd be the wise thing to do. I was mounted an' away 'fore Sheriff Galbraith had even left his law office. I rode northwards for two days an' two nights with scarcely a pause.'

'You feared pursuit?' said the mayor.

'I sure did, Mr Lucas. The further from Tuscarora I got, the happier I felt. Which is how I fell in with Two-gun an' Jake. I called in at a small way-station on the Idaho-

Oregon border, where I ordered a meal an' a glass of beer. Guess I was still pretty nervous an' kept glancin' towards the door, 'cause Two-gun an' Jake, who were sittin' at the bar, came over an' asked me why I was on the run. I tried to deny it, but, in the end, I told 'em my story. They, in turn, informed me they were both outlaws, specializin' in holdin' up banks. It seems they would do the actual robbery, while a lookout kept watch outside. However, on their last raid, things had gone drastically wrong. They themselves had only jest succeeded in escapin', while their lookout had gone an' got hisself shot. Consequently, they were in need of a new lookout. They offered me the job.'

'An' you took it?' exclaimed Rebecca.

'No. But neither did I turn it down. Hell, I was a fugitive from justice, wanted for a murder I hadn't committed! I was real scared I'd be overtaken an' either killed or captured. I figured, therefore, that I'd feel a deal safer in company. So, I said, if 'n' they'd let me ride along a ways with 'em, I'd consider their proposition.'

'An' they agreed?' said Lew Jackson.

'They did. An' a few days later we came across Rebecca strugglin' with that red savage who had abducted her.'

'For which both she an' I are eternally grateful,' declared Lucas.

'Yessir,' said Lew Jackson. 'However, your story does sorta present me with a problem, Mr Malone.'

'How so?' asked the young Texan.

'Wa'al, I guess you're still wanted for murder.'

'It was no murder. I told you the facts an'–'

'That's for a court to decide.'

'But–'

'I believe you. Nevertheless, as a law officer, I oughta arrest you an' convey you back to Tuscarora, where you'd stand trial...'

'An' git hanged.'

'Billy's right!' cried Rebecca. 'That sheriff'd make absolutely certain that he's convicted.'

'Quite so,' said Lucas. 'There is no question of you handin' Mr Malone over to the authorities in Tuscarora. Rebecca an' I clearly owe him a debt that can never be repaid. You must forgit what's been said. Erase the entire story from your mind.'

'I dunno. It ain't–' began the deputy.

'Come, come, Lew. It's not as if you've actually got a "Wanted" notice on Mr Malone,' snapped Lucas.

'I might have,' said Lew Jackson obstinately. 'Back in the law office, there's a whole heap of "Wanted" notices.'

'One of which may, or may not, refer to Billy. Surely you need take no action meantime?' remarked Rebecca.

'I s'pose not,' said the deputy.

'Yeah. Wa'al, for the present, I reckon we'd best remain on the same side,' stated Billy Malone.

'Whaddya mean?' asked Lew Jackson.

'I mean, we're a long ways from home. An' look!'

The young Texan pointed. The others

turned their heads. From their vantage point above Freedom Falls, they could clearly discern the trail wending its way through the Blue Mountains. And, to their dismay, they observed, some two or three miles off, a band of Indians riding northwards towards them.

'Injuns!' exclaimed Lew Jackson.

'Are they the same band that attacked Moose City, do you think, Pa?' cried Rebecca nervously.

'Those goddam Snakes led by Crazy Fox? I guess so,' replied the mayor.

'Then, let's git the Hell outa here!' exclaimed Billy Malone.

'Yes. Let's do jest that,' agreed Lucas.

Hurriedly, they mounted their horses and began the difficult descent to the trail beneath. All four accomplished this without mishap and, thereupon, set off along the fork that headed due west.

They were a long way from the John Day river, but the trail was well defined and easy to follow. Also, it was downhill all the way.

Billy Malone and the girl were both refreshed after their night's sleep, and fear of the Indians had, for the moment, caused them to forget the hunger in their bellies. They rode like the wind, with the mayor and the young deputy galloping along at their heels.

It was late morning before they eventually dropped down out of the foothills and onto the plain. Whether the Indians remained on their trail, they did not know. However, all of them strongly suspected that Crazy Fox and his braves were not too far behind.

They wound their way through the clumps of sagebrush that dotted the plain, until presently they reached the river. Further south it was much wider and shallower. There were plenty of places that could easily be forded. But, in the north, it was far too deep. They would have to cross at Jingle's Ferry.

The ferryman's cabin and the ferry itself soon hove into view. However, of the ferryman there was no sign. They expected him to appear at the door of his cabin at any moment, but he did not. Consequently, they reined in their horses, then quickly dismounted and hitched the animals to the rail outside the cabin.

'I wonder where in tarnation the feller is?' muttered Andrew Lucas, as still the ferryman failed to put in an appearance.

'Mebbe he's asleep?' suggested Lew Jackson.

'At this late hour!' rasped Lucas.

'Wa'al, let's go find out,' said Billy Malone, and he led the way into the cabin.

It was dim, almost dark, inside, for the shutters remained closed, and what little light there was filtered in through the narrow gaps in those shutters. Having just come in from the bright sunlight outside, it took some moments for their eyesight to readjust and for them to properly observe their surroundings. The first to do so was Rebecca.

'Oh, no!' she screamed.

The others followed the girl's horrified

gaze and found themselves staring at the ferryman propped up in a chair at the far side of the cabin. His shirt front was soaked with blood, his face was deathly white and his eyes stared sightlessly into space. He had been shot twice in the chest and was stone dead.

''Mornin', folks.'

They immediately spun round, to be confronted by the menacing figures of Two-gun Danny O'Hare and Jake Rough. O'Hare's pair of pearlhandled British Tranters and Rough's Remington were clutched in the outlaws' hands and aimed directly at the four newcomers.

'What the blazes...?' began the mayor, but O'Hare cut him short.

'So, we meet again,' said the gunman. He leered wickedly at the girl and snarled, 'Guess we got ourselves some unfinished business, huh, Miss Lucas?'

'No, no! I–'

'You ain't got no business with my daughter,' snapped Lucas. 'If you're lookin' for a reward for savin' her from the clutches of that stinkin' redskin, then that's fine. I'll be happy to settle. However, there's a condition.'

'Oh, yeah?'

'Yeah. You don't lay a finger on her.'

O'Hare glanced at his companion and then both men laughed harshly.

'I don't think you're in any position to lay down conditions. Am I right, Jake?' rasped O'Hare.

'Right,' averred his bearded accomplice.

'But—'

'But nuthin'. We dictate the terms.'

'No!'

'Yes. If'n' you an' the gal an' your deppity marshal wanta survive, you'll do exactly as I tell you.'

'What about me?' cried Billy Malone.

'Aw, you ain't gonna survive,' retorted O'Hare. 'Me an' Jake don't take kindly to fellers who double-cross us.'

'We sure don't,' concurred Rough.

'You – you cain't jest kill him in cold

blood!' exclaimed Lew Jackson.

'No; no, you cain't!' screamed Rebecca.

'Jest you watch me,' grinned O'Hare.

At that very moment, however, there was a loud thud against the cabin door.

'What the Hell?' growled Jake Rough.

'You, deppity marshal. You're nearest. Open the door,' commanded O'Hare.

Lew Jackson hesitated, then slowly stepped across and pulled open the door. Protruding from it was an arrow.

'Looks like Crazy Fox has left his callin' card,' drawled the young deputy marshal.

SEVEN

The Snake Indians sat upon their horses in a long single line, facing the cabin. In the centre of the line was Crazy Fox, with the gnome-like, grey-haired Fire Lance on his right hand. They watched intently as the door slowly opened. A few moments passed and then Jake Rough poked his head out.

'Whaddya want?' he cried nervously.

Crazy Fox, who spoke no English, said a few brief words, which Fire Lance speedily translated.

'Crazy Fox wants the girl. Also, the three men who killed his brother.'

'How in tarnation does he know there was three of us?' muttered Two-gun Danny O'Hare from inside the cabin.

'Like that feller, Stone,' growled Rough, 'they probably read the tracks.'

This remark reminded O'Hare that the man named Stone was no longer with his erstwhile companions. Where had the fellow disappeared to, he wondered? But O'Hare had more pressing matters to attend, if he and Rough were to escape from Jingle's Ferry with their scalps still attached. He promptly dismissed all thought of Stone from his mind.

'Tell Crazy Fox that we'll happily hand over his brother's killers an' the girl. Also, there's a crate of whiskey that he can have.'

Jake Rough shouted out this message and then waited while Fire Lance repeated it in his native tongue to Crazy Fox. After a short consultation between the two Indians, Fire Lance again spoke.

'Crazy Fox asks what you want in exchange?'

'Only our lives,' replied Rough. 'We realize we ain't got no chance of escapin', that you could simply attack an' kill us all. But you'd lose a few braves in so doin', for we'd certainly put up a fight. This way, you git what you want an' me an' my pardner save our scalps. Whaddya say?'

Another consultation followed, then Fire Lance cried, 'Bring out the three men and the girl.'

Inside the cabin, O'Hare grinned wickedly.

'OK, folks,' he snarled. 'You heard what the Injun said.'

'You – you propose handin' us over to them red savages?' exclaimed an incredulous Andrew Lucas.

'No! You cain't be serious!' said Billy Malone.

'Please, Mr O'Hare, Mr Rough, don't do this! Let's forgit what's past. After all, we're all white folks,' pleaded Rebecca.

'We'll all die if we attempt to hold out,' said O'Hare. 'There ain't no way we're gonna defeat Crazy Fox an' his braves. There's jest too darned many of 'em.'

'Wa'al, we could try. This cabin's pretty solid. It should be easy enough to defend,' remarked the deputy.

'Should it?' O'Hare laughed harshly. 'All them Injuns gotta do is bombard us with flamin' arrows. They'd soon smoke us out.'

'I ain't so sure,' muttered Lew Jackson.

'Wa'al, I am. So, git movin'.' There was a malevolent gleam in the tall, rake-thin gunman's eyes as he added, 'Either you folks step outside now, or me an' Jake start shootin'.'

'I don't think he's kiddin', my dear,' said Lucas, taking hold of his daughter's arm and propelling her gently towards the door.

'But, Pa, what will the Injuns do to us?' sighed Rebecca.

'I don't rightly know,' confessed the mayor.

'We ain't got no choice, anyways,' said Billy Malone. 'This coupla murderin' bastards'll shoot us dead unless we do what they demand an' step outside.'

'That might be preferable to...'

'While there's life, there's hope, Rebecca.'

'I s'pose, Billy.' But Rebecca did not sound at all convinced. And, as she, her father, Billy Malone and the young deputy marshal walked out into the sunshine, she cried out, 'These three men didn't kill your brother, Crazy Fox. It was—'

''Course it was them,' yelled O'Hare, suddenly appearing in the doorway beside his pal, Jake Rough. 'They was boastin' 'bout it not ten minutes ago.'

'That's right, Two-gun,' affirmed Rough. 'They sure was.'

Rebecca opened her mouth to protest further, but Crazy Fox held up his hand and, glaring furiously at her, silenced her with the sheer malevolence of his look. He turned to Fire Lance, who translated what both Rebecca and O'Hare had said. Crazy Fox listened, his black-painted face cold and impassive.

Then, he spoke briefly. Fire Lance translated. 'Crazy Fox says for the woman to be quiet. He knows full well that his brother, Dancing Fox, was killed by her three companions.'

Two-gun Danny O'Hare suppressed a

smile. Rebecca's present companions were three in number. She had been rescued from Dancing Fox by three persons. Ergo, her present companions and her rescuers must be the same three men. To convince Crazy Fox otherwise would be extremely difficult, if not impossible.

He and Jake Rough remained in the doorway of the cabin while the Indians rode forward, dismounted and surrounded the quartet. Ignoring their protests, the braves stripped them of their arms, bound them with whipcord and heaved them up onto their horses. Then Crazy Fox assigned one brave to lead each of the captives' horses by the bridle.

His coal-black eyes flashed angrily as he addressed the four. He spat out his words with unconcealed venom. Yet again Fire Lance translated.

'We return to our camp where tomorrow we bury Dancing Fox with due honour. Afterwards, we attend to you. The woman will provide sport for my braves. As many as

want her shall have her. Then we shall skin
and scalp all four of you before we kill you.
You shall die slowly and in great pain.'

As Fire Lance spoke, the colour faded
from the faces of the four prisoners and
Rebecca gasped, 'I think we should have let
Mr O'Hare an' Mr Rough shoot us.'

'Don't despair, my dear,' replied her
father. 'We may yet escape. Ain't that so, Mr
Malone?'

'Yes, Mr Lucas, it is,' said the young
Texan, although in fact he feared the worst.

As for Lew Jackson, he merely looked
glum and said nothing.

A few short words from his chief
prompted Fire Lance to utter a second
demand.

'You promised us whiskey,' he cried.

O'Hare and Rough exchanged glances.
O'Hare regretted having made that
promise, for he felt that he could have
struck the same deal without it. When he
had mentioned the whiskey, however,
O'Hare had been extremely anxious to

present Crazy Fox with an offer he could not refuse. Now it was too late. He dared not go back on his word.

'There's a crate inside, containin' a dozen bottles,' he said sourly. 'I'll go fetch it.'

The whiskey had belonged to the ferryman, for he was sometimes obliged to provide board and lodging for the passing traveller. O'Hare hefted the crate and carried it to the door. He dumped it down just outside the threshold, then stepped back inside the doorway.

'There y'are,' he rasped.

Crazy Fox barked out an order, and twelve of his braves hurried forward and each grabbed a bottle from the crate. As they leapt back into the saddle, he barked out a further order and the entire band, complete with their four prisoners, turned and galloped off in a cloud of dust towards the foothills.

Crazy Fox himself was the last to leave and, before he did so, he quickly drew his Colt Peacemaker and blasted off four shots at the men in the doorway. Just in time, they dived out of sight, the bullets ripping into the door, which they hastily shut behind them.

When, some minutes later, Two-gun Danny O'Hare inched open the cabin door and cautiously peered out, Crazy Fox and his band of renegade Snake Indians had vanished into the sagebrush.

'Thank God!' he sighed. 'Those goddam red savages have gone!'

Jake Rough stuck his ugly, bearded countenance round the doorpost and grinned broadly.

'Y'know, Two-gun, I was scared stiff those pesky redskins were gonna attack us,' he confessed.

'Wa'al, Crazy Fox did his darnedest to kill us.'

'But, if'n' they'd rushed the cabin...'

'Crazy Fox'd've lost several of his braves. An' he'd already got what he'd come for, or thought he had. So, why bother attackin' us?'

'Anyways, I'm sure glad he didn't.'

'Me, too, Jake,' concurred O'Hare. 'It's a pity, though, that Crazy Fox caught up with us, for I really fancied sportin' with that li'l blonde.'

'An' then there was the ransom we could've demanded off her father.'

'Yeah.'

The two outlaws stepped out into the sunlight. The couldn't make up their minds whether they were pleased or not. On the one hand, they had lost both the girl and the chance to make a great deal of money. On the other hand, they were still alive.

It was as they strolled nonchalantly towards the hitching-rail and their horses that the big man suddenly rode out of the sagebrush. He rode up to within fifteen yards and then reined in his bay gelding.

'Howdy, fellers,' said Stone. 'We meet again. Only this time there ain't no point in lyin' to me.'

'How – how long have you been hidin' in that there brush?' demanded O'Hare.

'Long enough to witness you coupla yeller-bellied bastards handin' over those four white folks to Crazy Fox an' his braves.'

'We – we didn't have no choice,' retorted Rough.

'No?'

Stone coldly eyed the gunmen. He was furious that he had not arrived earlier, in time to rescue Rebecca and the others from the two desperadoes. A stupid error had prevented him. Not being too familiar with the territory between the Blue Mountains and the plain, the Kentuckian had tried to cut through what he took to be a ravine, only to discover that it was a box canyon. Consequently, he had had to retrace his steps for several miles and had reached Jingle's Ferry some minutes after the arrival of Crazy Fox and his war-party.

'Look, we ain't got no quarrel with you,' said Jake Rough, anxious to avoid any confrontation, for he sensed that the big Kentuckian was liable to prove a formidable adversary. Even odds of two to one in his and O'Hare's favour did little to reassure him.

'Wa'al, mebbe I've got a quarrel with you,' drawled Stone.

'Don't push this, feller,' hissed O'Hare, his mean black eyes as cold and hard as pebbles, and his hands hovering menacingly above the pearl handles of his British Tranters. Unlike his companion, he feared no man.

'You heard Two-gun,' added Rough. 'So – so jest back off.'

'I don't think so.'

There followed a moment or two of utter silence, while Stone and the two outlaws stared coldly at each other. Then, all at once, the three of them went for their guns.

Stone fired twice, leaping from the saddle as he did so. His first shot whipped the stovepipe hat from O'Hare's head and his second struck Rough in the left shoulder. As for the outlaws' first shots, O'Hare's whistled past the Kentuckian's right cheek and Rough's missed by a foot or more.

Stone's sudden leap threw the two gunmen off balance and, before they could recover and loose off any further shots, he pumped two slugs into each of them.

Two-gun Danny O'Hare was hit in the chest and knocked flat on his back. And Jake Rough took one bullet in the throat and the other in the left temple. The latter bored a neat hole in Rough's skull and exploded out of the back of his head in a cloud of bone splinters, blood and brains.

The Kentuckian reloaded the Frontier Model Colt and coolly surveyed his victims. That Jake Rough was dead there was no doubt whatsoever. But Danny O'Hare still breathed, albeit extremely shallowly, Stone stood over him and took careful aim. His seventh shot entered the plumb centre of O'Hare's forehead and killed him instantly.

Stone smiled grimly. It had been sheer bad luck that Rebecca Lucas had jumped from Running Fox's clutches straight into those of the two desperadoes he had just killed. Their young companion's intervention had saved her from rape at their hands, but now she was again in deadly danger, as were her father, her rescuer and Moose City's young deputy marshal. And the odds were stacked against Stone effecting their rescue. He had counted the Indians as they sat astride their horses in a line facing the ferryman's cabin. There had been seventeen of them, including their leader. Stone guessed there had to be more, for he assumed Crazy Fox had detailed some of his war-party to take his brother's body back to their camp. So, what should he do?

The sensible move would be to head for Fort Franklin and alert the bluecoats. Which thought suddenly reminded the Kentuckian that he had seen neither hide nor hair of Lieutenant Freeman and his troop since they parted company on the previous day. What, he wondered, had become of them? They had been in hot pursuit of Crazy Fox and his braves. Stone feared the worst. He had specifically warned the subaltern against riding into a trap, and yet their non-appearance seemed to indicate that that was exactly what Freeman and his men had done. Stone cursed and decided against the sensible move.

The Kentuckian figured that, by the time he reached Fort Franklin, it would be too late to save Rebecca and the others. He and the soldiers could never hope to reach Crazy Fox's hideaway in time. He would, therefore, have to go it alone and damn the odds.

Stone stared bleakly up at the Blue Mountains. Hidden somewhere in that vast wilderness was the Snake Indians' camp. He remounted his bay gelding and set out to follow their trail.

It proved relatively simple to track them, for the Indians had no notion that they were being followed. Last time, they had deliberately made it easy for Lieutenant Freeman and his troop to pursue them, with the intention of leading the soldiers into a trap. This time, however, their ignorance of Stone's presence caused them to be plain careless.

The Kentuckian rode cautiously up through the foothills into the vast forest that cloaked the lower reaches of the mountains. It was a tortuous trail that he followed, through ravines, across streams and on and on, ever upward.

Dusk was falling when, upon cresting the rim of yet another ravine, Jack Stone found himself peering down into a small hollow. On one side of it, a path wound its way from its floor up to the ravine's edge, while, on the other three, sheer rock-faces rose up to the bounds of the surrounding forest. Stone swiftly dismounted and, hiding both himself and his horse behind a tumble of boulders, eagerly surveyed the scene below.

There were six tepees pitched in a circle round a camp-fire on which a deer was roasting. One tepee was much larger than the rest, and it was in front of this that the Indians had staked out their four prisoners. They were each stretched upon the turf, in the form of a Saint Andrew's cross, with wrists and ankles tied to pegs driven into the ground. The braves were dancing round them, screeching and laughing, while Crazy Fox and the ancient tracker, Fire Lance, stood in the doorway of the large tepee, watching impassively. Of the deceased Running Fox there was no sign. Stone conjectured correctly that he was laid out on a bier inside the large tepee.

As Stone watched, one of the braves suddenly left the dancing circle and confronted Crazy Fox. He shouted a few harsh words, gesturing, as he did so, towards the prostrate form of Rebecca Lucas. Crazy Fox's eyes blazed and he struck the brave with a blow so savage that it sent him crashing backwards through the circle of dancing braves to land with a thud on his back. Crazy Fox glared at the young warrior and addressed him in a low yet menacing monotone.

'W – what's goin' on?' cried Andrew Lucas, from his prone position, for the brave had almost landed on top of him.

'Crazy Fox has decreed that only after the

funeral of his brother should his braves sport with the woman,' explained Fire Lance. 'But young Striped Tail wants the woman now and said so. It was foolish of him, for Crazy Fox does not tolerate such questioning of his orders.'

'No.' Lucas watched as the young brave staggered to his feet, nursing his bruised jaw. 'Guess he don't at that,' he muttered.

At this point, Crazy Fox snapped out another command and the Indians' dance ended abruptly. The braves, thereupon, headed towards the campfire, where they set about carving up the roasted deer. Crazy Fox and Fire Lance joined them, and they all squatted down round the fire and began to eat the meat.

Jack Stone felt the pangs of hunger gnawing inside his belly, as he crouched on the rim of the ravine and watched the Snake Indians wolfing back great chunks of the succulent roast venison. This was one torture that did not affect Rebecca and her three companions. The prospect of rape, mutilation and a lingering, painful death had completely robbed them of their appetites. To free them from their stakes was going to be no easy matter. Stone realized he would have to wait until the light had finally faded completely.

The Indians, meantime, had begun to drink the whiskey which they had taken from Jingle's Ferry. This, Stone felt, was a good sign, since the red man was reputed to be prone to drunkenness. The consumption of too much whiskey by Crazy Fox and his braves would surely be to the Kentuckian's advantage.

As the light continued to fade, the eating ceased, but the drinking continued unabated. More and more of the ferryman's red-eye was consumed and, as the hours passed, the Indians became drunker and drunker.

Although there was a clear, starlit sky, Stone would still have had some difficulty observing the scene below, had it not been for the light cast by the camp-fire. This illuminated the hollow to a certain degree and, consequently, Stone was able to discern the effects the alcohol was having upon the redskins. Some collapsed into a stupor beside the fire, while others staggered off and disappeared inside one or other of the tepees. A few tottered across to where the four white folks were staked out and spent a little time taunting them, before they, too, headed unsteadily towards their tepees. Finally, only two remained conscious beside the camp-fire. Crazy Fox and Fire Lance sat for a while longer, then eventually rose to go. But they were by no means sober as they made their way back to the largest of the six tepees.

On passing their prostrate prisoners, Crazy Fox snarled a few words at them, which Fire Lance translated: 'Tomorrow you die!'

Thereupon, the renegade chief and his veteran tracker vanished inside the tepee and silence reigned over the camp.

Stone continued to wait. He wanted the Indians to all be in a deep sleep before he ventured down into the hollow. He noted that Crazy Fox had appointed no sentries to watch over his hideout. Whether this was because the Indian arrogantly assumed there was no chance of pursuit, or whether it was due to carelessness, as a result of his having consumed rather too much whiskey, Stone did not know. Nor did he care.

When, presently, the Kentuckian reckoned that it was as safe as it was ever likely to be to descend into the hollow, he quietly rose to his feet. He had no means of knowing what time it was, but guessed that it was probably one or two o'clock in the morning.

He took hold of the reins of his bay gelding and tied them to the branch of a single stunted tree growing nearby. Then he pulled the Winchester from his saddle-boot and checked both it and his Frontier Model Colt, to ensure that they were loaded. This done, Stone turned and began, slowly and cautiously, his descent of the path down into the hollow.

EIGHT

Jack Stone reached the foot of the path without mishap. He paused and listened. The only sounds to be heard were the raucous snores of the sleeping Snake Indians and the occasional hoot of an owl from the surrounding forest. Taking great care, he made his way to the camp-fire, which consisted now of only a few burning embers. There were six or seven braves sprawled in the grass around it.

Stone approached the nearest of these braves and, reversing his Frontier Model Colt, bent over and dealt the Indian a sharp blow to the back of the skull. Having laid him unconscious, the Kentuckian thereupon removed the knife from the brave's belt and proceeded across the hollow to where Rebecca Lucas and the others lay staked to the ground.

'What the...?' began Andrew Lucas, as the dark figure loomed over him.

'Ssh!' hissed Stone, adding in a whisper, 'It's me, Stone.'

'Gee!' gasped the mayor, then immediately lapsed into silence.

The other three, too, had the good sense to remain mute.

Stone crouched down and began to saw through the whipcord binding Rebecca to the stakes. When he had freed the girl, he straightaway began to work on her father's bonds, then proceeded to release Billy Malone and, finally, Lew Jackson.

'Come on,' whispered the Kentuckian, as he severed the last cord. 'Let's go git your hosses.'

He had earlier observed that the horses, both the Indians' and those belonging to their captives, were hobbled at the far side of the encampment. Therefore, taking care not to disturb any of the sleeping braves, he led the girl and the three men past the camp-fire and across to where the horses stood. Their saddles lay on the ground nearby and, by the light of the stars, they each found his or her own and began, as quietly as possible, to saddle up.

Once this was achieved, Stone motioned that they should follow him. He again skirted the camp-fire, his companions walking behind him in single file and leading their steeds by the bridle.

When they reached the foot of the path that wound its way upwards to the ridge overlooking both the hollow and the neighbouring ravine, Stone paused and turned to Andrew Lucas who was immediately behind him.

'You carry on,' he murmured. 'But take care, for it's a tricky climb.'

'You ain't gonna lead us, then?' enquired the mayor.

'Nope. I'll bring up the rear,' said Stone.

He stood to one side and, while the others began their ascent, kept a watchful eye on the Indians' camp, his Winchester held cocked and ready to fire.

The climb was made with remarkably little noise, certainly not enough to disturb the slumbering redskins. Stone prayed that they might reach the rim unobserved, and be several miles away before any of Crazy Fox's band awoke and discovered their prisoners had escaped. However, it was not to be.

Andrew Lucas had just reached the summit and Lew Jackson, the last of the four, was approximately forty feet from the top of the path when the front flap of the largest of the six tepees was flung open and the ancient tracker, Fire Lance, staggered out. He was obeying a call of nature, but instantly forgot that need upon spying the erstwhile captives clambering up the winding path.

'Stir yourselves! The white men and the girl are escaping!' he cried, and he rushed across to the camp-fire and kicked the nearest brave hard in the ribs.

As he did so, Jack Stone fired. The

Kentuckian's shot struck Fire Lance in the chest and hurled him backwards a good six feet. The first three of the Indians to stagger drunkenly to their feet met with a similar fate. Stone fired off three more shots in quick succession, with deadly effect, the slugs ripping into the braves' bodies and sending them crashing to the ground.

All was in chaos in the Snake Indians' camp, as Stone turned and quickly followed his fellows up the winding path. Upon reaching the top, he immediately unhitched his bay gelding and leapt into the saddle. The others also swiftly mounted.

'Which way?' enquired Billy Malone.

'Down out of these goddam mountains,' said Andrew Lucas.

'No,' said Stone. 'We try a run down to the plains an' we're dead for sure.'

'How so?' enquired the mayor.

'Wa'al,' replied the Kentuckian, 'I cain't see us outrunnin' them Injuns nohow.'

'Mebbe not. But–'

'If'n' we're overtaken, we've got only two

guns with which to try an' fight 'em off: my Winchester an' my Colt.'

'So?'

'There's 'bout twenty of 'em.'

'That's right. We won't have a goddam chance!' interjected Billy Malone gloomily.

'Not if we head downhill. Now uphill we might jest find us a vantage point from which we can hold 'em off till help arrives,' said the Kentuckian.

'Help! An' where in tarnation are we gonna git help?' cried Andrew Lucas.

'There's that troop of bluecoats under the command of Lieutenant Freeman. They was hot on the Injuns' trail when we last saw 'em. Mebbe they'll turn up,' suggested Lew Jackson.

'If they ain't already been massacred,' said Lucas.

Stone smiled grimly. When he set out from Jingle's Ferry, this very thought had crossed his mind. In which case, there would be no aid to come. Nevertheless, he did not know for absolutely certain that this had happened.

'It's our best hope,' he rasped. ''Deed our only hope.'

'Mr Stone's right,' declared Lew Jackson, 'an' I know a spot 'bout six miles east of here, where we can mebbe hold 'em at bay for a li'l while. It's a rock formation, on top of a high ridge, that's known as Fort Wolf on account it looks kinda like a fort from one angle an' like a wolf's head from another.'

'Then, lead on, Deppity,' said Stone.

'Yeah. Let's git the hell outa here!' cried Billy Malone.

And so they set off in the wake of the young deputy marshal, who, having been born and bred in that part of the State of Oregon and having hunted with his father in the Blue Mountains, knew the territory almost as well as any Snake Indian.

Although Lew Jackson was right and the rock formation known as Fort Wolf was only six miles away, it took them more than two hours to reach it, so difficult was the terrain they had to traverse. Upon reaching it, they rode in amongst the boulders, then dismounted, hobbled the horses and settled down to wait. Although they had neither heard nor seen any sign of pursuit, Andrew Lucas doubted whether they had thrown Crazy Fox and his war-party off their tracks.

'Where the blue blazes are them red varmints?' he muttered nervously.

'I guess they'll be a li'l ways behind us, for they was pretty drunk,' drawled Stone.

'Too drunk to follow our trail, mebbe?' said Rebecca hopefully.

'I doubt that,' said Billy Malone. 'Drunk or sober, those savages are gonna be thirstin' for our blood. An' they'll find us, believe me.'

'Yeah. I'm afraid Billy's right,' confirmed Stone. He handed the Winchester and a case of shells to the deputy marshal. 'You take the rifle, Deppity,' he said. 'I'll use the Colt.'

'For how long d'yuh think you an' Lew will be able to hold 'em off?' asked Rebecca, with an anxious smile.

'Dunno, miss,' replied Stone.

'I mean, hopin' that troop of US Cavalry is gonna turn up an' save us is bein' kinda optimistic, ain't it?' commented the girl.

'Yeah; it's one helluva long shot,' agreed her father.

'Wa'al, sometimes a long shot comes off,' growled Stone.

'If it don't, we're surely done for,' declared Lew Jackson.

'Then let's pray that it does,' sighed Rebecca.

Her four companions heartily endorsed this sentiment, and they prepared themselves for the inevitable arrival of the redskins.

The ferryman's whiskey had undoubtedly added greatly to the chaos in the Indians' camp. Shocked and thrown into confusion by Jack Stone's sudden rescue of their captives, the Indians would probably have quickly rallied, had they been sober. Their drunkenness, however, had thrown them into total disarray.

Crazy Fox had watched aghast while first the old tracker and then three more of his braves were shot down by Stone. The starlight had afforded Crazy Fox a pretty good view of the Kentuckian, as he followed the others up the winding path. But since the Snake chief had emerged from the tepee with only a hunting-knife on his person, he had been quite unable to do anything to prevent Stone's escape.

Instead, he had sought to gather together his braves and organize an immediate pursuit. No easy task. Whether Indians are more susceptible to strong liquor than their white counterparts is debatable. The fact remains, however, that Crazy Fox's renegade band were in no state to mount a pursuit. A few were capable of clambering into the saddle, but the majority could scarcely stand. Indeed, it took Crazy Fox over an hour to sober them up sufficiently for them to give chase. And then the Indians made the mistake of heading downhill, in the direction of the plains, on the natural assumption that their fleeing prisoners would make for home.

The distance to be covered between the Indians' mountain lair and the safety of the nearest township, either Moose City or nearby Caxton, was so great that Crazy Fox was confident he and his men would over-take their quarry before they could reach either settlement. Also, with each mile covered, his braves' condition improved, as the effects of the drink continued to wear off. And, so, Crazy Fox gradually increased the pace of the pursuit.

They had ridden about four miles, when, upon reaching some high bluffs, Crazy Fox halted the chase and rode to the cliffs' edge. From this eminence, he was afforded a fine view of the way ahead. The trail wound its way down through the surrounding forest, appearing like a silver ribbon in the bright starlight. Crazy Fox stared at this vista with some consternation. Of his quarry there was absolutely no sign. Yet the trail was in full view for several miles ahead. Surely they could not be that far in advance? And, if they were not...?

As he pondered this question, the young brave named Striped Tail galloped up. He had been left behind when the band rode out, for he had drunk rather more whiskey than most. He did not join the others, but rode straight over to where his chief sat astride his horse on the rim of the bluffs.

'Aha! So, you come at last, Striped Tail!' snarled Crazy Fox.

'Yes. You – you had gone when I mounted and left the camp,' said the brave.

'So?'

'So, I – I studied the tracks to – to find out which way you had gone.'

'Downhill, of course. It is unthinkable that the white men and the girl would climb higher into the mountains.'

'Is it?'

'What do you mean, Striped Tail? Are you saying that they did?'

'Yes, Crazy Fox.'

The Indian Chief looked hard at the

young brave. Striped Tail had been Fire Lance's protégé and had learned from the veteran all the old tracker's skills.

'The white man's tracks – did they lead upward, then, into the mountains?' demanded Crazy Fox.

'They did. I – I observed them while I was looking for yours. They – they ran in the opposite direction.'

Crazy Fox scowled. The white folks had done the unthinkable. His eyes blazed and his cruel features looked grimmer than ever. He recalled the big man who had evidently freed his captives. Was it he who had fooled the Indians by making such an unexpected move? Crazy Fox reckoned that it probably was, and he there and then determined to have vengeance upon the big man.

'You have done well, Striped Tail,' he rasped, whereupon, without more ado, he set off back the way he had come.

Striped Tail promptly followed and, after a few moments' hesitation, the rest of the war-party wheeled round and galloped off in his wake.

It was, therefore, somewhere between four and five in the morning, and dawn was breaking, before Crazy Fox and his band eventually approached within rifle range of the rock formation on top of which Jack Stone and his party lay hidden. They, for their part, held their breath, hoping against hope that the Snake Indians would ride on by. But it was not to be. Both Crazy Fox and Striped Tail spotted their quarry's tracks. Immediately, Crazy Fox gave the command to charge, and the entire band came whooping and hollering up the short incline towards Fort Wolf

Lew Jackson's first shot toppled Striped Tail from the saddle, while his second struck another brave in the chest. As he brought a third hostile crashing to the ground, Crazy Fox and the rest of his band pulled up, turned and fled. None had succeeded in coming within range of Jack Stone's Frontier Model Colt.

They halted and re-grouped just out of

range of the young deputy marshal's rifle. From the safety of the rocks, Stone and his companions watched as Crazy Fox harangued his braves.

'I guess Crazy Fox is urgin' 'em to try another frontal attack,' said Lew Jackson.

'They don't seem none too keen, though,' remarked Billy Malone.

'Nope,' said Stone.

'While our ammunition lasts, I reckon we can hold 'em at bay,' declared Lew Jackson confidently.

'Mebbe,' said the Kentuckian.

'There's ravines on either side of Fort Wolf. It can only be approached along that there ridge. So, the Injuns' sole option is a frontal attack,' argued the deputy.

'That's right,' agreed Andrew Lucas. 'They cain't mount an attack from the rear, 'cause, to git there, they'd need to pass directly beneath these rocks, an' they'd be sittin' ducks.'

'I figure they've got a coupla options,' retorted Stone. 'They can mount a full-

blooded frontal assault an' hope to over-
whelm us by sheer force of numbers, or they
can wait till nightfall an' then creep up on us
under cover of darkness.'

'They surely won't wanta wait till nightfall? Hell, it's only jest daybreak!' exclaimed
Billy Malone.

'D'yuh reckon Crazy Fox has got that
much patience?' enquired Lucas.

'Wa'al, if'n' they attack in daylight hours,
he knows he's gonna lose some more braves.
An' he cain't afford to lose many more, not
if he wants to remain on the warpath,'
drawled Stone. 'So, me, I figure he'll choose
the second option.'

'Then, what do we do? Jest sit it out?'
growled Lucas.

'That's all we can do. Like we decided
earlier, we wait for help to arrive,' said the
Kentuckian.

'If it ever does,' muttered Lew Jackson.

'Leastways, we got 'bout fourteen hours
'fore those varmints attack,' declared Stone.

In the event, he was right in assuming that

160

the Indian leader would choose the second option. Crazy Fox, on finding his followers reluctant to mount a second assault on Fort Wolf, reflected on the situation and reluctantly came to the conclusion that he had best delay that assault until after nightfall. To attempt another daylight attack would, he ruefully decided, cost too many Indian lives.

Consequently, no attack was mounted, though Crazy Fox and his braves made a stream of individual forays to a point just beyond the range of Lew Jackson's Winchester. Each brave in turn would detach himself from the main body of Snake Indians and gallop furiously forward, shouting defiance at his hidden enemy and brandishing either lance or rifle. By so doing, the redskins hoped to provoke the white men into wasting some of their limited supply of ammunition.

This worked only once. Lew Jackson loosed off a couple of shots, which fell short of their target. A few sharp words from Jack

Stone followed and, thereafter, the young deputy refrained from responding to the Indians' provocation. Nonetheless, Crazy Fox and his braves persisted in making these defiant gestures for a further two hours.

Whether they would have continued for a third hour will never be known, for, as Crazy Fox mounted a fifth personal charge, cries of shock and alarm rent the air behind him. He promptly pulled up his racing pony and swivelled round in the saddle. At the same moment, a volley of shots rang out and half-a-dozen braves toppled from their horses. Then a bugle sounded and the surviving Indians turned about and returned fire. The prayers of Jack Stone and the others had been answered: the US Cavalry had arrived.

In the ensuing exchange of shots, Crazy Fox's braves were cut down like wheat before the scythe. Only four survived the murderous fusillade issuing forth from the approaching soldiers. Those four immediately abandoned their position and rode forward to join Crazy Fox.

To escape the bluecoats, the Indians had perforce to pass beneath the towering rocks of Fort Wolf. And the trail took them well within range of both Lew Jackson's Winchester and Jack Stone's Frontier Model Colt. Yet they had no choice other than to take that trail. Behind them were the soldiers, ahead the peaks of the Blue Mountains. They simply had to make for the peaks, if they wished to survive.

Crazy Fox led the dash for freedom and, as he galloped madly past Fort Wolf, a bullet from the Winchester parted the feathers in his head-dress.

A second grazed his left shoulder, but he continued to ride hell for leather, and, moments later, he had passed the rock formation and was once again beyond the reach of the deputy's rifle.

His four followers were rather less fortunate. One was struck in the skull by Lew Jackson's third shot and killed instantly, the bullet blasting his brains out.

The next two fell victim to Jack Stone's revolver. Slugs of .45 calibre ripped into them and knocked them backwards out of the saddle. As for the fourth of Crazy Fox's braves, his horse lost its footing, stumbled and threw him. Then, as he staggered groggily to his feet, simultaneous shots from the deputy marshal and the Kentuckian smashed into his chest and finished him off.

When the soldiers met up with the valiant defenders of Fort Wolf, it seemed it was not merely a troop of US Cavalry that had ridden to their rescue, but in fact an entire company, led by none other than the commander of Fort Franklin, Lieutenant Colonel John Coburn.

'Gee, are we glad to see you!' exclaimed Andrew Lucas.

'Yessir!' echoed Lew Jackson.

'But we didn't expect you, Colonel. We thought that mebbe Lootenant Freeman an'–' began the mayor.

'Lootenant Freeman's dead,' said the colonel. 'He an' his troop rode into an ambush. Only Sergeant McGill here an' a coupla others survived.'

'How – how did you find us?' gasped Rebecca.

The stocky, grey-haired colonel smiled kindly at the girl and explained.

'Sergeant McGill led us to the scene of the ambush an' then Blueshirt took over.' Coburn indicated the stone-faced Indian who sat mounted beside him. 'He's a full-blooded Cheyenne an' the best goddam tracker in the territory.'

This was a bold claim, but, since both Fire Lance and Striped Tail were dead, it was probably true.

'Wa'al, it seems you annihilated the whole goddam renegade band,' said Lucas.

'With the single exception of Crazy Fox hisself,' growled McGill.

'That's quite right, Sergeant,' interposed the company's second-in-command, Lieutenant Tom Strang, and, turning to his commanding officer, he asked eagerly, 'Can I take some men an' pursue that stinkin', murderin' savage?'

Coburn studied the young subaltern with an appraising eye. Lieutenant Tom Strang, a slight, blond-haired young man of twenty-three, had trained at West Point with the late lamented Hugh Freeman, and the two men had been posted together to Fort Franklin. They had been boon companions, and it was clear to the colonel that the subaltern was desperate to avenge his friend's death. Well, Coburn mused, the demise of such a dangerous hostile was essential for the peace of the territory. While Crazy Fox lived, he posed a threat to every white settler in the State of Oregon.

'Very well,' said Coburn. 'Take Sergeant McGill and half-a-dozen troopers an' go hunt down the miscreant.'

'Yessir!'

The zealous young lieutenant wasted no time, but straightway detailed six troopers to accompany him and set off in the wake of the Snake Indian. The troopers, no less keen than their officer to kill Crazy Fox, followed at a furious gallop, while Sergeant Joe McGill brought up the rear.

The trail ran for several miles along a high ridge, snaking ever upward into the mountains. On the longer stretches, Strang and his men were able to spot the Indian ahead of them on the trail, but then he would suddenly vanish round a bend. They continued to ride at full pelt, and it seemed that they were gradually gaining upon the redskin. Ahead of them, Crazy Fox, no longer the pursuer, was experiencing what it was like to be hunted down.

The chase proceeded for a couple of miles more, whereupon the trail began to make a rapid descent into a narrow defile, with precipitous grey stone cliffs on either side. Since there was no way Crazy Fox could have turned off, the soldiers, when they reached it, plunged straight into the mouth of this gorge.

Lieutenant Strang and his party were forced to reduce their pace since the floor of the gorge was strewn with boulders. It twisted and turned its way deep into the mountains. Then it came to an abrupt halt, its far end being blocked by an enormous rock-face. The gorge was in truth a box-canyon, similar to the one into which Jack Stone had strayed on his way to Jingle's Ferry

The soldiers gazed in amazement at the cliffs facing them, for of Crazy Fox there was no sign.

'Where in tarnation has that red devil gone?' enquired one trooper.

'He cain't've jest vanished into thin air!' exclaimed a second.

'Cain't he? Then, where the hell is he?' demanded a third.

For some moments Lieutenant Strang looked about him in disbelief

'Wa'al, Sergeant, what do you make of it? Do you think Crazy Fox actually entered this gorge?' he asked.

'He had to. There was no way round it,' replied McGill.

'But—'

'Let's back-track, sir. An' keep our eyes peeled,' suggested McGill.

'Very well. Lead on, Sergeant.'

Joe McGill rode slowly at the head of the column. He took careful stock of both sides of the gorge as he trotted along. And so it was that he spotted the narrow crevice in the left-hand cliff-face. Had it not been that, on his way into the gorge, he was concentrating wholly upon the path ahead, he would surely have observed it earlier. He rode over to it while the lieutenant and the troopers waited.

McGill urged his horse forward. The crevice was just wide enough to admit a horse and its rider. McGill rode through the narrow gap and found himself inside a large, gloomy cavern.

'Goddammit!' he snarled.

A moment or so later, he rejoined his comrades.

'Wa'al?' said the subaltern.

'I reckon Crazy Fox holed up in there until we'd ridden past, an' then simply rode back the way he came.'

'To what end?' demanded Strang. 'There was no way off that ridge till way past the spot where we surprised him an' the rest of his band.'

'So?'

'So, Sergeant, he's gonna ride slap-bang into Colonel Coburn an' the others.'

'I doubt that, sir. By the time Crazy Fox reaches that spot, both our company an' the civilians will surely have left an' be on their way back down towards the plains. All Crazy Fox has to do, therefore, is make sure he doesn't catch up with 'em. Then, at the first opportunity, he can break away from the trail an' slip into the surroundin' forest.'

Tom Strang scowled darkly.

'Which means the sonofabitch will be free, to continue his campaign of murder, rape an' plunder!'

'Not without men at his back, sir,' declared McGill.

'He will recruit them.'

'From the reservation?'

'Yes.'

'He's jest lost an entire war-party. I don't see many young bucks bein' keen to follow a leader with his record.'

'No?'

'No, sir.' McGill smiled grimly. 'I sure as hell would've liked to have caught up with the murderin' bastard. But, at least, his days as a renegade chief are over. I don't figure we'll ever hear of him again. He'll jest disappear into the Blue Mountains.'

'I hope you are right, Sergeant,' said Strang, but the young lieutenant did not sound entirely convinced.

NINE

While Lieutenant Tom Strang, Sergeant Joe McGill and their detail were pursuing Crazy Fox, both the civilians and the soldiers at Fort Wolf were, as McGill conjectured, on their way down the mountains. Only two soldiers had been wounded in the encounter with the Indians, and they but slightly. Both, having had their wounds tended, were able to mount and ride.

The journey back to Moose City could not be completed that day. An overnight stop, down amongst the foothills, was deemed necessary. There the civilians gladly shared the soldiers' provisions. And then, at crack of dawn on the following day, the company set off once more.

Colonel Coburn and his men parted from the civilians a mile or so outside Moose City and, while Andrew Lucas, Jack Stone and the others headed towards the township, the soldiers veered off in the direction of Fort Franklin.

It was early afternoon when the quintet finally rode across the town limits and into Moose City's Main Street.

The first person to spot them was the Reverend Martin Ross, just as he was leaving the church.

'Andrew!' he cried delightedly.

His cry was followed almost immediately by one from Doc Barton, standing on the stoop in front of the Lucky Strike Saloon, and another from the rancher Dale Stewart, who was in town to pick up provisions.

Then, within minutes, the street was filled with citizens eager to welcome the mayor and his companions. Amongst the first to arrive on the scene was Naomi Lucas. She experienced a joyous and tearful reunion with her daughter and husband while the crowd cheered. Then Andrew Lucas mounted the steps in front of the mayor's office and addressed the assembled throng.

'Fellow citizens!' he cried. 'Let me tell you here an' now that Crazy Fox's war-party has been wiped out.' This statement brought forth further cheers, and Lucas had to wait for them to die down before continuing, 'Crazy Fox alone escaped, but was hotly pursued by a detail of Colonel Coburn's soldiers. Indeed, I expect I shall shortly hear from the colonel that the murderin' sonofabitch has been killed or taken.'

'Let's hope he's taken. Shootin's too good for him,' yelled Dale Stewart.

'Yeah; I'd sure like to see the red devil dancin' on the end of a rope,' declared Lawrence Baird.

'Me, too,' added Doc Barton enthusiastically.

Several other townsfolk made similar comments, before eventually Andrew Lucas succeeded in quietening them and proceeding with his address.

'Wa'al, folks,' he said, 'it's been one hell of an adventure, an' have I got a story to tell!

However, for the moment, I don't feel like no more speechmakin'. There are one or two matters need attendin' to, an' then I propose to head home. Before I step down, though, let me say a lot of you folks have been a deal less fortunate than me. You lost loved ones when them danged Snake Injuns attacked Moose City, an' I want you to know that you all have my heartfelt sympathy. I – I can say no more. Thank you.'

So saying, Lucas turned and shepherded his wife and daughter into the mayor's office. He paused on the threshold and indicated to his three fellow adventurers that they, too, should join him. And, once they were all inside, he spoke.

'Gen'lemen,' he said, 'how can I possibly repay you?'

Lew Jackson stared at the mayor in surprise.

'But, Mr Lucas, I was jest doin' my duty!' he exclaimed.

'What you did went well beyond the bounds of duty, Lew,' said Lucas. 'And, as for you, Mr Malone...'

'Billy,' said the young Texan.

'Billy. As for you, wa'al, I shudder to think what would've happened to Rebecca if'n' you hadn't intervened.'

'I couldn't do no other,' replied Billy Malone.

'Even so.'

'I don't want no reward.'

'You could offer Billy a job, though,' suggested Rebecca. 'If – if you'd like one, Billy?' she added diffidently.

'Sure would,' said the Texan. 'I'd like to quit runnin', mebbe settle down an' sink some roots. An' this here town seems a pretty good place to do jest that.'

'Pa, couldn't you help?'

'Wa'al...'

'Your cousin Fred has that hoss ranch a coupla miles outside town. He's lookin' for a wrangler,' said Naomi Lucas to her husband. Then, turning to Billy Malone, she enquired, 'You any good with hosses?'

'Yes, ma'am,' he declared confidently.

'That's settled, then.'

Andrew Lucas opened his mouth to say something, but he was forestalled by Lew Jackson.

'Er ... I – I don't wanta spoil things, but – but it's gonna be kinda difficult if Billy stays,' he stammered.

'Whaddya mean?' demanded Lucas.

'Wa'al,' said the young deputy, looking decidedly uncomfortable, 'Billy is a wanted man.'

'What?' cried Naomi.

'You tell Mother the story, Billy,' said Rebecca.

'OK.'

Billy Malone smiled wryly and thereupon began to relate the story he had earlier told Rebecca, her father and the deputy on the hilltop above Freedom Falls. When he had finished, Naomi scratched her head and said, mystified, 'So, what's the problem, Lew?'

'The problem is, I'm a peace officer sworn to uphold the law.'

'Yeah?'

'I cain't pick an' choose who I arrest. If someone's wanted by the law, whoever he may be, I've got a duty to arrest him.'

'Aw, come on, Lew!'

'Lew's right, Mrs Lucas,' interjected Stone.

Naomi faced the big Kentuckian.

'You a law officer, Mr Stone?' she demanded.

'I have been in my time.'

'An' you figure it's Lew's duty to arrest Billy?' cried Rebecca.

'I didn't say that exactly,' replied Stone. 'If'n' Billy was jest passin' through, I guess Lew could turn a blind eye. But, should he stay, wa'al'

'I take your point, Mr Stone,' said Lucas. 'So, what do we do?'

'We don't know for sure that Billy is a wanted man,' said Rebecca.

'I cain't imagine that there ain't a warrant out on him,' said Lew Jackson.

'Neither can I,' agreed Billy Malone. 'If

179

what I was told back in Tuscarora is true, an' there was no reason for the folks to lie, then Sheriff Bernie Galbraith is certain to have put out a "Wanted" notice.'

'Wa'al, let's be quite sure,' said Stone.

'Yes,' said Rebecca, more in hope than in expectation. 'Let's do that.'

'OK,' agreed the deputy. 'I gotta whole heap of "Wanted" notices back in the office. We'll mosey on over there an' take a look at 'em.'

This suggestion met with everyone's approval, and, a few minutes later, they were all ensconced in the law office, with Lew Jackson riffling through a thick pile of papers.

Suddenly, he stopped riffling and picked up one of the notices. He studied it carefully and then glanced at Billy Malone.

"This feller you shot; his name was Donald Galbraith, right?'

'Right.'

'That's odd.'

'Whaddya mean, odd?'

180

'Wa'al, Billy, it says here that Donald Galbraith was murdered by a certain Billy Smith of Lubbock, Texas.'

'I – I don't understand!'

'You from Lubbock, Texas, Billy?' enquired Stone.

'Nope. I hail from Texas sure enough, but not from Lubbock. I come from Laredo.'

The Kentuckian laughed.

'Sheriff Bernie Galbraith may be the roughest, toughest peace officer in the entire State of Nevada, but he sure as hell ain't the smartest,' drawled Stone.

'Whaddya mean?'

'I mean, Billy, he's been duped.'

'By who?'

'By your trail boss, I guess.'

'Mr Somers?'

'Yup.' Stone grinned and went on to explain, 'The way I figure it is this: Nobody in Tuscarora knew Billy. So, when you lit out, the sheriff had no option but to git your details off your boss. Mr Somers evidently ain't no fool. He knew there was every

181

chance that the folks in the saloon had heard your companions addressin' you as Billy. An' I guess he reckoned that your Texas accent would've been noted, too. So, he simply gave the sheriff a false surname an' a different home-town in Texas.'

'Which means I don't feature on no "Wanted" notice!'

'That's right,' agreed the Kentuckian.

'Which, in turn, means that I've got no reason to arrest you,' said Lew Jackson.

'Nope.'

'So, you can stay, Billy!' exclaimed Rebecca delightedly.

'Yup.'

'Wa'al, I gotta say I'm darned pleased that's sorted itself out the way it has,' declared the young deputy marshal, and he and Billy Malone promptly shook hands

'Come on, Billy,' said Rebecca. 'I'll take you out to the hoss ranch an' introduce you to Cousin Fred.'

'Before you go,' said Andrew Lucas, 'I propose a small celebration this evenin'. In view of all the recent deaths in the town, a public celebration would certainly not be appropriate. However, a small private party to celebrate our safe return would not, I think, be out of order. You are, therefore, all invited to dinner at our house this evenin'. Shall we say at seven? Would that be all right, my dear?' he asked, turning to his wife.

'Perfectly,' replied a smiling Naomi.

Thereupon, the six split up. Rebecca and Billy Malone set off towards the horse ranch, watched by Rebecca's parents and Jack Stone, who had all stepped outside onto the sidewalk. Deputy Marshal Lew Jackson, meantime, attended to his duties inside the law office.

'If'n' we're gonna have folks round this evenin', I guess I'd best head on home an' start preparin',' said Naomi.

'Yes, my dear, I s'pose you had,' replied the mayor. He continued to stare after his daughter and her companion. 'I hope we've done right, encouragin' Billy Malone to stay on here in Moose City,' he mused.

'Why do you say that, Andrew?' enquired his wife.

'It's jest that we don't know very much 'bout young Billy.'

'No; that's true.'

'An' I git the impression that Rebecca's kinda sweet on him.'

'That's hardly surprisin', considerin' he saved her life.'

'Yes; that's quite a story, all of which I'll tell you later. But, even so, I had hopes she might one day marry one of the two Stewart boys or mebbe Luke Baird. An' now...'

'Rebecca's only seventeen. She won't be marryin' anyone for a while yet. So, let's jest allow events to take their natural course.'

Andrew Lucas pondered this suggestion.

'I s'pose so, my dear,' he said, finally. Then, as Naomi headed for their fine two-storey house, which was on the edge of town opposite the church, the mayor turned to Jack Stone and asked, 'How about you, Mr Stone, do you plan stayin' on here in Moose City?'

'I guess not,' drawled the Kentuckian. 'I'm headin' south an' mebbe lookin' up an ole pal in Nevada.'

'You ain't got no firm plans, then?'

'Nope.'

'So, how about if'n' I offered you the post of town marshal?'

'But, Lew...'

'He's kinda young and inexperienced. Sure, Ben Langley was groomin' him to take over when he retired, but that was gonna be some years ahead.'

''Fraid I ain't interested,' said Stone, adding pointedly, ''Sides, from what I've seen of young Lew Jackson, he'll make a darned fine marshal. An' you owe him.'

'Yeah. Yeah, I reckon I do.'

'He's actin' marshal at the moment.'

'Sure, but his post will need to be confirmed. An', if he is formally appointed, then we'll have to find a new deppity.'

'So, confirm him in the job an' find a new deppity.'

'It ain't up to me alone. It's a town council decision.'

'But you're mayor, an' if you back Lew, he'll surely git the job?'

'I guess.'

'So, forgit Lew's age. He won't let you down, I'm certain he won't.'

'Yo're right!' declared Lucas. 'I – I will nominate him.'

'Good!'

'But, what about you, Mr Stone?'

'Me?'

'Yeah. I owe you, too.'

'I ain't lookin' for no reward, Mr Lucas.'

The mayor smiled and, pulling out his wallet, from the inside pocket of his black city-style jacket, he extracted a wad of ten-dollar bills and offered it to the Kentuckian.

'I know you ain't lookin' for no reward,' he said. 'But I'd take it as a personal favour if you'd accept this small token of my gratitude.'

'Wa'al...'

'Please, Mr Stone.'

Stone shrugged his broad shoulders and took the money. He had no wish to offend the mayor and, besides, it would certainly come in useful as he travelled south.

'Thank you, Mr Lucas,' he said.

'No; thank you, Mr Stone,' replied the mayor.

TEN

The party that evening at the Lucas home was an undoubted success. In addition to Jack Stone, Billy Malone and Lew Jackson, the mayor had invited the Reverend Martin Ross and Lawrence and Margaret Baird and their three children. The wine and the conversation flowed, Naomi's food was excellent, and the euphoria generated by the lucky escape of the mayor and his friends, ensured that it was indeed a joyful occasion.

As the Reverend Martin Ross put it: 'We must thank God for your deliverance and safe return, and rejoice that the threat posed by those red renegades is no more.'

Jack Stone had planned an early start on the following morning, and so he bade everyone farewell that evening. This was just as well, for, when he set out at the crack of dawn, Moose City was still asleep. The only person to see him on his way was the town's acting marshal, Lew Jackson.

The youngster stood upon the sidewalk outside the law office and continued to watch until, eventually, the Kentuckian disappeared from view.

A mile or so out of town, Stone fell in with a small detachment from Fort Franklin under the command of one Captain John Sanderson, a hard-bitten professional. The soldiers were on their way south to meet up with a pay-wagon, which they intended to escort back to the fort.

Captain Sanderson had not taken part in the rout of Crazy Fox's war-party, but had been left in command of Fort Franklin in the absence of his colonel. He was, therefore, interested to hear Stone's first-hand account of the incident.

'And, so,' concluded the Kentuckian, 'with the single exception of Crazy Fox hisself, every man jack of 'em was killed.'

'Yes; it was unfortunate that their leader should escape,' commented the captain.

'He was pursued by some of your men,' drawled Stone. 'I don't s'pose you know whether they succeeded in capturin' him?'

Sanderson grimaced.

'No; they did not,' he said.

'Crazy Fox eluded them?'

'I'm afraid so. Lootenant Strang an' his detail returned to the fort jest as we were leavin'. He told me that the sonofabitch had given 'em the slip.'

'Godammit!'

'That's what comes of sendin' a greenhorn in pursuit of a wily warrior like Crazy Fox,' growled Sanderson. Stone noted the bitterness in the man's voice and guessed that the captain felt he should have been included in the foray against the renegade Snake Indians. 'That company that got itself wiped out a few days back, it was under the command of another greenhorn, Lootenant Freeman,' Sanderson added morosely.

'Yeah.'

'Colonel Coburn ain't by no means the most competent commander I've ever served under,' concluded the captain, though in a low whisper so that his men did not hear.

'Guess not. Still, he an' his men did save me an' Mayor Lucas an' the others,' replied Stone.

'Yup. Pity 'bout Crazy Fox though,' said Sanderson.

Thereafter, for several miles, they rode in silence. It was pretty wild territory that they traversed, for the trail wound its way through hill country, across various streams and one river, and into and out of several tracts of wood and forest.

When, eventually, they re-emerged onto the plains, Captain John Sanderson breathed a sigh of relief

'That was a big sigh,' remarked the Kentuckian.

'Wa'al, I'm kinda relieved to be out in the open once more,' confessed the soldier.

Stone glanced round at the troopers riding

in column of twos behind them. There was a round dozen of them.

'You surely didn't fear an ambush, Captain?' he probed. 'I mean, it'd have to be a pretty darned large war-party that'd take us on; an', with the annihilation of Crazy Fox's band...'

'I know; there ain't no reports of any other renegade outfits in the territory'

'Exactly.'

'Nonetheless, I got the distinct feelin' that we were bein' spied on.'

Stone smiled grimly.

'Hmm, yes; I know what yuh mean,' he said.

'You git the same feelin'?'

'I must confess, Captain, I did.'

Jack Stone had often, during his colourful and dangerous life, depended upon his animal instincts for survival. Consequently, he was likely to sense danger where other men might not. And, on several occasions during the ride from Moose City, he, too, had felt in his bones that someone was watching the detail as it proceeded southwards along the trail. The question was: who was the watcher watching, Captain Sanderson and his men, or him, Stone?

'Let's jest keep our eyes peeled,' said the captain.

'OK.'

The two men did exactly that, but to no purpose, for nobody hove into view. They continued to follow the trail across the plains, and the feeling that they were being watched gradually faded.

Presently, just as dusk was beginning to fall, the small prairie town of Seneca came in sight. Captain Sanderson determined to press on south, but Stone had no pay-wagon with which to rendezvous, and, therefore, a mile outside Seneca, he parted company with the soldiers and headed off towards the town.

Seneca was like a hundred other prairie townships spread across the West. It boasted one Main Street, and that was it. There were only two two-storey buildings. They were situated opposite each other on Main Street. One was the Powder-horn Saloon and the other the Plains Hotel.

Jack Stone carefully surveyed both before riding into the nearby livery-stables and handing over his gelding and his saddle into the care of the ostler. Then, carrying his Winchester, which he had removed from the saddle-boot, he made his way along the sidewalk towards the Plains Hotel.

The hotel was a great deal grander than most to be found in the West. It was built in the style of a cotton plantation owner's mansion, with a fine balustraded balcony that ran the whole length of the upper floor and could be reached at both ends by a wooden staircase rising from the sidewalk. The hotel was owned by a southerner, but not by one of the south's elite. Art Hamilton was a poor southerner, who had headed north, struck it lucky at cards and, with his winnings, built the Plains Hotel in that flamboyant style so beloved by the southern gentry.

Stone would normally have sought rather less expensive accommodation, but, with Andrew Lucas's wad of ten-dollar bills in his pocket, he determined to spend the night in the relative luxury of the Plains Hotel. He had, perforce, to pay in advance, for, since the bedrooms all had french windows leading out onto the hotel balcony, Art Hamilton was taking no chance that his guests might decide to leave without settling their accounts.

The room on the upper floor was large and airy and well appointed. The bed was extremely comfortable and the bed-linen of a quality the Kentuckian had rarely encountered.

He ordered a bath and a shave, and afterwards enjoyed an excellent supper in the hotel restaurant. Then, puffing on a fine Havana cigar, also purchased at the hotel, he headed across the street, intent upon sampling the pleasures on offer at the Powder-horn Saloon.

This establishment was jointly owned by

Horace Boyd and Laura Wyndham. Theirs was strictly a business partnership. Horace Boyd was in his mid-sixties and had never had much interest in women, while Laura Wyndham admitted to thirty, but was nearer forty, and had for the past twenty years worked various saloons as a sporting woman. They operated well as a team and had built an extremely run-down saloon into a prosperous business. The Powderhorn Saloon boasted several gaming tables, a piano-player and a bevy of attractive saloon girls. These girls were managed by Laura who, these days, rarely offered her services, and then only to a few old and valued customers.

The two partners could not have been more dissimilar in looks.

Horace Boyd was a small, wizened figure with a bald head, a thin, bony frame and a distinct squint in one eye. He was invariably clad in a dark city-style suit, together with either a green or a red brocade vest; and he wore a pair of gold-rimmed spectacles perched on the bridge of his thin, beaky nose.

Laura Wyndham, on the other hand, was a tall, seductive blonde, with a ripe, voluptuous figure which forever threatened to burst out of the tight confines of her low-cut midnight-blue velvet gown. Her face was pretty rather than beautiful, and her best features were undoubtedly her wide, sensuous mouth and mischievous blue eyes.

On the night that Jack Stone entered the Powder-horn Saloon, the bar-room was already pretty full. He pushed open the bat-wing doors and threaded his way through the tables and the crowd to the bar with its hammered copper bartop. There were two bartenders in action and, so busy was it, Horace Boyd was helping them out. It was he who served Stone.

'What can I do for yuh?' he enquired, bestowing upon the Kentuckian what he considered to be his most professional smile. This made him look like a particularly dyspeptic crow, which accounted for the fact that his customers had long nicknamed him 'Caw-Caw'.

'I'll have a beer, thanks,' said Stone.

'Jest ridin' through, stranger, or are yuh plannin' to stay awhile in Seneca?' enquired the saloon-keeper.

'Jest ridin' through,' said Stone.

'Ah!' Horace Boyd continued to smile as he poured the beer. He was of a naturally curious nature and liked to know everything about everybody in town. 'Your beer,' he said, finally.

'Thanks.'

Stone paid for the drink and, while he slowly sipped the beer, glanced round the bar-room. He had bathed, shaved and eaten, and now he was enjoying a fine cigar and a glass of beer. All he needed to complete his evening was an accom-modating woman. Yet the Powder-horn Saloon's sporting women were all very young and reminded Stone too much of Sadie Juniper. Although accustomed to witnessing and sometimes causing violent deaths, Stone had been both shocked and saddened at the young red-head's sudden and unexpected demise. He had, therefore no wish to be reminded of it.

These thoughts were flitting through the Kentuckian's mind when his gaze chanced to rest upon the seductive figure of Laura Wyndham. He smiled broadly. The blonde was exactly what he was looking for. Experienced and sensual, and nothing like the late lamented Sadie Juniper.

It was at this moment that the bear-like Butch Boone entered the saloon, shouldered his way through the crowd and approached the blonde. Boone was a giant of a man, with an ugly bearded face and the foulest of tempers. He owned a run-down homestead a couple of miles out of town and had a wife and children whom he terrorized. He was frequently drunk and invariably abusive, and was hated and feared by the entire population of Seneca. His visits to town were abhorred by everyone, and, in particular, the town marshal and his two deputies, who always had the un-enviable task of subduing the giant home-steader.

As Boone stepped up to Laura, her diminutive partner came from behind the bar and bravely intervened.

'I – I thought I told yuh I – last time, Boone, that – that you weren't w – welcome in the Powder-horn,' stammered Horace Boyd nervously.

Butch Boone turned and glared at the little man.

'You gonna throw me out, Horace?' he demanded.

'Wa'al. I – I–'

'You ain't got the guts.'

'The marshal b – banned you. He – he said you was to confine your drinkin' to – to Whiskey Joe's place,' protested the saloon-keeper.

This was true. A month earlier, Butch Boone had badly injured one of the saloon girls and then smashed up several tables and chairs before the law arrived upon the scene. Whereupon, threatened by the marshal's shotgun, the drunken homesteader had eventually been subdued and marched off to jail. Subsequently, he had been released and told to restrict his drinking in future to Whiskey Joe's, a disreputable drinking-den on the edge of town, frequented by Seneca's rougher elements. Now, it seemed, Boone was proposing to break that embargo.

'I don't give a damn what that pesky marshal said,' he retorted and, turning to Laura, he snarled, 'I want one of your girls, an' I want one now!'

It was evident that Boone had consumed more liquor than was good for him, probably at Whiskey Joe's, and that he was in no mood to be thwarted. Nevertheless, Laura had no intention of submitting any of her girls to his tender mercies.

'Last time you was here, you hurt young Lily, an' you hurt her pretty badly,' said Laura.

'So?'

'So, Mr Boone, the gals are off limits as far as yo're concerned. Permanently off limits.'

'In that case, Miss Laura, I'll have you,' rasped Boone, and he grabbed the blonde by the arm, digging his fingers so hard into her flesh that she cried out.

'L – let her go!' yelled Horace Boyd.

'Make me.' Boone glared round the bar-room. The games of chance had been temporarily suspended. All eyes were focused upon him and the blonde. 'Any of you yeller-livered sonsofbitches man enough to try?' he demanded loudly.

The drinkers at the bar promptly looked away or dropped their gaze, while the gamblers turned again to their cards or dice.

'I – I'll send for the marshal!' declared Boyd, white-faced and trembling.

'You do that an' I'll break Miss Laura's arm,' replied Boone, with a wicked grin.

The saloonkeeper blanched.

'N – no! No! I–' he began, when a voice from immediately behind his left shoulder interrupted him.

'I don't think you're gonna break anyone's arm.'

Boyd turned to face the speaker. What he saw was a big, tough-looking fellow in a buckskin jacket, the stranger who was just riding through. Jack Stone had left his unfinished beer and cigar on the hammered copper bar-top and stepped forward to join the two partners and their unwelcome guest.

Butch Boone glowered at the Kentuckian. Stone was big, but he was bigger. A couple of inches taller and a good three to four stone heavier, he reckoned. He was right in this calculation, though he had not taken into account the fact that the extra stones were composed of excess flab rather than muscle.

'Yuh know, stranger,' he sneered, releasing his hold on Laura's arm as he spoke, 'it ain't wise to stick your nose into other folks' affairs. If'n' yuh do, yo're liable to git taught a pretty severe lesson.'

'Really?' said Stone and, without warning,

he rammed a fierce left hook hard into Butch Boone's belly.

The sheer speed and power of the Kentuckian's punch took the drunken giant by surprise, knocked the wind out of his sails, and doubled him up.

A split second later, Stone caught Boone on the point of his jaw with a tremendous right uppercut. The force of this blow lifted Boone clean off his feet and hurled him backwards, to land with a resounding thump on the bar-room floor, a thud so thunderous that it seemed to shake the entire building.

Butch Boone lay flat on his back, his arms and legs spreadeagled. He was quite motionless.

'Holy cow! You – you've killed the big bastard!' exclaimed one of Horace Boyd's customers.

'Aw, what a shame! He was such a nice feller,' said Stone and, shrugging his broad shoulders, he returned to the bar and took a long, satisfying puff at his cigar.

'Wa'al, I cain't have his body litterin' up the place,' said Boyd. 'Will some of you fellers take him over to the funeral parlour? There's a beer in it for you.'

It took four of the Powder-horn Saloon's patrons to lift and carry the inert form of Butch Boone outside. They paused for breath on the stoop and, as they did so, the town marshal appeared on the scene.

Explanations followed and then the marshal instructed the four to lay Boone down on the stoop. He crouched down beside the motionless giant and examined him. When he had finished, he grinned and peered up at the four men.

'Butch ain't dead,' he announced. 'He's jest out for the count!'

'Gee! Wa'al, I sure wouldn't wanta be around when he comes to!' exclaimed one of the four.

'Nor me. He'll be out for blood, for sure!' cried another.

'I don't think so,' replied the marshal. 'Not with a broken jaw, he won't.'

'His jaw's broke?'

'Yup. That feller must pack one helluva punch!'

'Jeeze!'

'Yeah. So, you fellers pick him up an' carry him over to the jail. We'll sling him in a cell an' I'll git Doc Donovan to have a look at him.'

So saying, the marshal turned and headed back the way he had come. The four men, thereupon, picked up their burden and followed in his footsteps.

Meantime, back in the saloon, Jack Stone was enjoying a large measure of Horace Boyd's finest whiskey. On the house.

This provoked one of Boyd's regulars to enquire, 'Hey, Caw-Caw! Ain't it gonna be drinks all round on the house?'

'The next time you punch Butch Boone on the jaw, Pete, I'll give yuh a whole bottle,' retorted the little man acerbically.

This remark brought forth guffaws of laughter from the other drinkers round the bar, and the man named Pete took his beer and departed in high dudgeon to the far end of the bar-counter.

'Wa'al, stranger, I sure owe you a vote of thanks,' said Laura Wyndham.

'That's OK, lady, it was my pleasure,' replied Stone.

'Call me Laura,' said the blonde, smiling warmly at the Kentuckian.

'OK, Laura.'

'An' what's your handle?'

'Jack.'

'Right, Jack. You stoppin' over?'

'For tonight, yes. Tomorrow I head on south.'

'Wa'al, if'n' yuh fancy a woman for the night, you can have the choice of any of my gals. Free.'

'That's mighty generous of you, Laura. You the proprietor of this here establish-ment?'

'Yup. In partnership with Horace.' Laura smiled and nodded towards Boyd. 'We're equal partners,' she added.

'Ah!'

'It's strictly a business arrangement, Jack.'

'In that case, Laura, how 'bout you sharin' my bed tonight?'

Laura stared in some surprise at the Kentuckian.

'You – you prefer me to one of them pretty young gals?' she exclaimed.

'That's right. I'm lookin' for someone who's both accommodatin' an' experienced.'

'Then I'm your woman.' Laura's bright blue eyes twinkled merrily and she continued, 'However, the beds upstairs ain't so very comfortable. Aw, they're OK for a quick tumble, but for an all-night session, wa'al...'

'Don't worry. I've booked me a room across the street in the Plains Hotel,' drawled Stone.

'That sounds jest dandy!' cried Laura and, turning to her diminutive partner, she said, 'Horace, me an' Jack here are gonna mosey on over to the Plains. So, gimme a bottle of your finest rye an' two glasses.'

'Comin' up.' Boyd, highly relieved that Butch Boone hadn't smashed up the saloon, was in an expansive mood. He handed the bottle to Stone and the glasses to Laura. 'Have yourselves a real good time!' he grinned.

'You bet,' said Laura.

Then, taking the Kentuckian by the arm, the blonde headed for the door.

Five minutes later, the couple were upstairs in the Plains Hotel and standing outside Stone's bedroom.

Laura Wyndham paused on the threshold while Stone went in and lit the kerosene lamps. Then she glanced round the room and murmured appreciatively, 'This matches anywhere you'd find in Frisco. 'Deed, I guess it's 'bout as classy as any of them swanky hotels back east!'

'I guess,' said Stone.

He stepped across to the small table set against the wall opposite the bed. Above this was a large rectangular mirror, while on it there stood a bowl and a water-jug. A chair was placed to one side of the table and, after first removing his Stetson, the Kentuckian pulled off his buckskin jacket and draped this over the back of the chair.

Laura, meantime, was testing the bed. The blonde threw back the covers and felt the mattress. She smiled, then, opening her reticule, she pulled out a two-shot derringer and quickly slipped it beneath the nearer of the two pillows.

'I'll sleep this side, Jack,' she said.

Stone turned and grinned.

'That's fine by me,' he replied.

'Good! Then come an' help me git outa this dress,' laughed Laura.

Dawn had broken when Jack Stone suddenly awoke. He glanced at the tousled blonde head and the full, firm breasts poking out above the bedclothes. He smiled. It had been one helluva night! So, what had wakened him? Pure instinct! The self-same instinct that had served him so well in the past and that, on the previous day, had warned him of an unseen watcher as he rode towards Seneca.

Stone shot up in bed and hastily glanced in the direction of the french windows, which, to his surprise, stood open. The early morning sun slanted in, and there, silhouetted within the frame of those windows, was the stocky, buckskin-clad figure of the Snake Indian renegade, Crazy Fox. The Indian's face was smeared with black war-paint, his fierce black eyes glinted venomously and he was aiming a Colt Peacemaker directly at the Kentuckian.

Crazy Fox transferred his gaze to Stone's Frontier Model Colt. It was in its holster, hanging by the gun-belt from the left-hand post at the foot of the big Kentuckian's bed. As for Stone's Winchester, it leant against the wall opposite the bed. There was no possibility that Stone could reach either gun before he, Crazy Fox, squeezed the trigger of his Colt Peacemaker. The Indian grinned wickedly.

He should not, however, have shifted his

gaze, for, in the split-second that he glanced away, Stone slipped his hand beneath Laura's, pillow and whipped out the derringer. In one lightning-fast movement, he aimed and fired. Both barrels struck Crazy Fox in the head, one bullet knocking out his left eye and the other drilling a neat hole in the centre of his forehead. The Indian toppled backwards onto the balcony, squeezing the trigger of his revolver as he did so. Three .45-calibre slugs buried themselves high in the wall above Stone's head. Then Crazy Fox crashed against and over the balustrade, and fell like a rock into the street below.

'Jeeze, Jack! What in tarnation's goin' on?' exclaimed Laura, shooting bolt upright in bed and gazing incredulously at the Indian as he fell from the balcony. 'Who the hell was that?' she demanded.

'Crazy Fox,' said Stone. 'He an' his band have recently been rampagin' across this territory. A coupla days back, I helped some white folks escape from his camp, an' later I was involved in the destruction of his war-party. He must've spotted me an' marked me down. Yup; I guess he came lookin' for revenge. Followed me as I rode south from Moose City.'

'But how'd he find you? He couldn't've known you was stayin' at the Plains, surely?' remarked Laura.

'I s'pose he was outside town, waitin' for me to ride out this mornin', an' thought he'd chance a quick *sortie* 'fore folks was up an' about. This hotel was the obvious place to look. Easy, too, with the balcony accessible from the street. If he hadn't found me here, I reckon his plan was to wait in ambush somewhere south of town, an' hope I was ridin' alone.'

While they were talking, the pair were hastily throwing on their clothes. Half-dressed, they hurried out onto the balcony and peered down at the street below. Crazy Fox lay spreadeagled in the dust. The shooting had roused Horace Boyd, one of his bartenders, a deputy marshal, Art

Hamilton, his clerk and his porter, several of Laura's sporting women and a couple of storekeepers. They all gathered in a circle round the fallen brave.

'My derringer. How'd yuh know it was under the pillow?' asked Laura suddenly.

'I saw you slip it there. In the mirror,' explained Stone. 'But, tell me, why d'yuh do that?'

'Force of habit, Jack. I was once robbed of a whole evenin's takin's. It happened some years ago an' the sonofabitch made off with a tidy sum. Ever since then, I've taken the precaution of keepin' a gun under my pillow.'

'You surely didn't s'pose I'd...?'

'No, Jack.' Laura smiled wryly. 'Like I said, it was force of habit. I stuck the gun there without thinkin'. It did occur to me afterwards to remove it, but, wa'al, the opportunity never arose. You kept me kinda busy.'

'Guess I did at that.' Stone chuckled and then declared, 'In the circumstances, it was jest as well you did slip that gun beneath your pillow.'

'Sure was,' smiled Laura.

They continued to peer down at the scene below. The deputy marshal, having examined the corpse, glanced up towards them and shouted, 'Who is this Injun?'

'He's named Crazy Fox,' replied Stone. 'An' I think it can safely be said that the last Snake Injun warrior has fought his final battle.'

This Large Print Book for the partially sighted, who cannot read normal print, is published under the auspices of
THE ULVERSCROFT FOUNDATION

Other DALES Titles
In Large Print

JANIE BOLITHO
Wound For Wound

BEN BRIDGES
Gunsmoke Is Grey

PETER CHAMBERS
A Miniature Murder Mystery

CHRISTOPHER CORAM
Murder Beneath The Trees

SONIA DEANE
The Affair Of Doctor Rutland

GILLIAN LINSCOTT
Crown Witness

PHILIP McCUTCHAN
The Bright Red Business

Other DALES Titiles
In Large Print

HAZEL BAXTER
Doctor In Doubt

JEAN EVANS
The White Rose Of York

J. D. KINCAID
A Hero of the West

ELLIOT LONG
Scallon's Law

LORNA PAGE
The Nurse Investigates

SALLY SPENCER
Murder At Swann's Lake

JACQUELYN WEB
The Lonely Heart